*A
Harlequin
Romance*

OTHER

Harlequin Romances

by ISOBEL CHACE

Many of these titles are available at your local bookseller, or through the Harlequin Reader Service.

For a free catalogue listing all available Harlequin Romances, send your name and address to:

HARLEQUIN READER SERVICE,
M.P.O. Box 707, Niagara Falls, N.Y. 14302
Canadian address: Stratford, Ontario, Canada N5A 6W4

or use order coupon at back of books.

SINGING IN THE WILDERNESS

by

ISOBEL CHACE

Harlequin Books

TORONTO • LONDON • NEW YORK • AMSTERDAM • SYDNEY • WINNIPEG

Original hardcover edition published in 1976
by Mills & Boon Limited

ISBN 0-373-01997-1

Harlequin edition published August, 1976

Printed in U.S.A.

...and Thou
Beside me singing in the Wilderness—
And Wilderness is Paradise enow!

The *Rubáiyát* of Omar Khayyám
(translated by Edward Fitzgerald)

CHAPTER I

Stephanie Black had never thought of herself as beautiful. On the contrary, she had long ago made up her mind that she was destined to be the practical support of her impractical father, a role that her delightful mother had never thought of as her own and was only too glad that her only daughter should take over as soon as she was old enough to do so.

Accordingly, Stephanie had looked after her parents' home from a very early age and, as soon as she had been old enough, she had taken a secretarial course and had begun to look after her father in his work as well. Desmond Black worked for an international company specialising in telecommunications and other similar products. He had never risen very high in the firm— Stephanie had sometimes thought that he had never wanted to—and nobody had been more surprised than himself when the company had landed a contract in Iran and he had been sent out to Isfahan to co-ordinate the work of laying the cables and supplying the necessary equipment.

Stephanie had gone with him. She had enjoyed the few weeks she had spent so far in Persia. There had been very little work to do and she had come and gone from their temporary offices as she had thought fit, languidly typing a few letters for her father whenever he had asked her to do so.

It hadn't occurred to her that her father should have been doing more. It takes time to settle in, he had told her, and she had believed him. At least, at first she had believed him, but as the days turned into weeks and *still* they seemed to be getting no further forward, she had become more and more concerned.

'We'll be here years if we don't get started soon,' she had reproached him.

'You enjoy yourself while you can,' he had answered. 'I know what I'm doing! Surely you don't doubt me, do you?'

Frankly, Stephanie did, but she was enjoying herself

7

too much to try to prod him into further action and had done a little less herself, and then hardly anything at all, until, in fact, that very morning when the blow had fallen. Her father was to return to the United Kingdom on the first available flight and, worse still, she was to stay on and work for his successor until the contract was fulfilled.

'But I've never worked for anyone else but you!' she had protested, more than a little upset by her father's grey face and—could it have been relief that the work had been taken out of his hands?

'Maybe, love, but officially you work for the company, not for me. As you know what's going on, it's reasonable that you should stay on with the next fellow. You'll probably like having more of a challenge than I was able to offer you.'

'I don't know that I can work for anyone else!' Stephanie looked at her father with something very like panic in her hazel eyes. 'It hasn't been like working at all being with you!'

'That's probably why I'm being sent home,' her father had returned gruffly. 'Will you keep on the apartment?'

'How can I? The new man will want it. It wasn't hired by the company for a mere secretary, but for the boss! I'll get a room somewhere—if I have to stay. But I'd much rather go home with you, darling!'

But her father had been unexpectedly firm about her staying on in Persia. 'Your mother and I will have to learn to manage without you some time,' he had said heavily. 'We depend on you far too much. Why, good heavens, Stephanie, *you* could have made a better job of getting this contract started than I have! The equipment hadn't arrived and I should have made a fuss about it sooner, but I was sure it would turn up in time—Oh well, no good crying over spilt milk, my successor will probably listen to you when you advise him to do something instead of letting things slide. I've been rather tired, though, recently. To be honest, I'm glad to be going back to England.'

All of which had only served to make Stephanie more than a little guilty. It was true that she had suggested that her father should have been more active, but she hadn't nagged at him until something had been done. She had been only too glad to follow his example and do next to nothing herself!

'They can't force me to stay!' she had repeated under her breath.

'No, dear, they can't. But I can, and I'm going to. It's time you had a life of your own, and you like it here. It won't be for long, but it will give us all the break we need. You're my daughter, Stephanie. I already have a wife and it's time we got to know each other all over again.'

Stephanie had been hurt. 'But Mother doesn't want to know—'

'Because you've done it all for her. A marriage is between two people and they have to make it work themselves. Not even their children can carry the burden for them. We've put upon you too much in the past, but you have your own life to live. It isn't right that you should try to live your parents' lives for them. I should have seen it before and perhaps I did, but I've always hated changes and having to make decisions that affect other people. It will do you good to get away from us for a bit and allow us to stand on our own feet without you. Will you stay for my sake?'

There had been nothing else to do but to give way. Yet now that she had time to think and to realise that she was going to be left behind in Persia, completely on her own, she acknowledged to herself that she was scared stiff. She had never worked for anyone else but her father, just as she had never lived anywhere but with her parents, looking after their comfort and cushioning them from the harsher realities of making ends meet and seeing that the bills were paid on time.

What would they do without her? Common sense told her they would muddle through somehow, but her whole being revolted at the chaos they would make between them of their daily life. Her father would never get to work on time, and her mother, charmingly vague as always, would turn night into day and sleep away the daylight hours without making any attempt to reduce the piles of washing-up that would await her in the sink.

Stephanie sighed, making an effort to put her parents out of her mind. Her father had been surprisingly effective on her behalf since he had made his decision to leave

9

her behind in Isfahan. He had arranged for her to have a smaller apartment in the same block where the company hired all its employees' accommodation, and had insisted on packing up his own things while she went out and spent her last afternoon of freedom before her new boss arrived.

'Buy your mother a small souvenir that I can take with me,' he had bade her, pressing a few notes into her hand. 'She'll like to know you thought of her. I'm afraid she'll take it rather badly that you haven't come home with me.'

'I'm still willing to come,' Stephanie assured him, hope rekindling that she might be able to persuade him after all.

'Your work is here,' he had insisted. 'Be off with you, my dear, and make the most of the last few hours you're officially working for me. Your next employer may not be so generous in giving you as much time off as I have. Not if he wants to keep his job,' he had added with a touch of bitterness. 'It always was beyond me, if the truth was known.'

And Stephanie had been unable to comfort him, because she had known that it was beyond him for the first day they had taken possession of the office the company had made available to them. Her father had been afraid of the problems the new telecommunications network had thrown up and, like the proverbial ostrich, he had hidden his head in the sand and hoped they would all go away while he was looking the other way.

In the end she had obeyed his wishes and had gone out, leaving him to do his own packing. The day was brighter than her mood and, for once, her surroundings failed to delight her. The first time she had seen Isfahan, she remembered, she had been overcome by its beauty. It was not only the buildings, magnificent as they were, it was something in the air, something even in the way the inhabitants walked and talked with an elegance not achieved elsewhere. Today, though, she scarcely noticed where she went, and was rather surprised to find that she had walked as far as the Maidan, the huge square where the Persians had once played polo in the days when Isfahan had been the capital city of the country.

Stephanie walked the whole length of the square, ignoring the covered maze of the bazaar at the end where she had come in, preferring to seek a gift for her mother at the other end where the Royal Mosque was situated and where there were a number of shops selling handmade artifacts of various types, all of them distinguished by the delicacy of which the Iranian is master.

She chose a nicely glazed pottery bottle decorated by a long-tailed bird in muted shades of grey and pink and blue. The owner of the shop wrapped it for her in a piece of paper, taking elaborate care to fasten it with string so that she could dangle the package from her fingers. When he had done, he bowed her out of his shop as if she had been visiting royalty and she didn't notice that at the same moment someone else was trying to come in. They met in the narrow doorway, jammed up against each other. The man took a quick step backwards, put both his hands beneath Stephanie's elbows and lifted her bodily out of the shop and on to the pavement outside.

Breathless, she became aware of his height and the solid impact of his body against hers. He had very bright blue eyes that sparkled in the sunshine and a mop of auburn hair that stood on end above an intelligent, bony face that appealed strongly to her. She found herself smiling up at him, her eyebrows raised in astonishment at his extra inches and the ease with which he had disposed of her.

'Goodness!' she said.

He grinned at her, his eyes amused. 'You were on your way out, weren't you?' he reassured himself.

'Yes, I was, though rather less precipitately. If you've broken my—'

'I haven't broken anything.'

She felt her mother's bottle with cautious fingers. 'No,' she agreed, 'but I'm beginning to know how the ball feels in a Rugger scrum.'

He laughed. 'How does it feel?'

She made a face at him and shrugged her shoulders. Nobody, but nobody, had taken such a liberty with her since she had been a small child and had appealed to every man who came to visit her parents to swing her right off the ground by her hands. She had grown out of such pleasures, of course she had, but she had been surprised to discover that there was still a childish bliss to be discovered in the helpless sensation of being swept off one's feet.

He took her package out of her hand, hooking the string round ths fingers and tucked her hand through his arm. 'What now, honey? Have you any more shopping to do?'

She made a tentative motion of withdrawal, but, when he didn't seem to notice, she changed her mind and spread her fingers on the fine texture of the cloth of the shirt he was wearing.

'I thought you were going inside?' she reminded him demurely.

'That was before I met you,' he returned, his gaze openly admiring her hazel eyes, the thick, dark lashes that surrounded them and which contrasted sharply with the pale gold of her hair, and the sweet, full lines of her mouth. 'What are you doing in Isfahan?'

She hesitated before answering, wondering who he was. She had never met anyone before who had given her such an instantaneous sensation of delight as this huge man. If she had been a child again, she would have yelled at him 'More! More!' exactly as she had then when she had wanted to be swung off her feet again. But she wasn't a child, and she had no business to feel like that.

'Are you a tourist?' she asked him abruptly.

'No, I'm here for a while. Is that what you're doing? Seeing the country?'

She shook her head. 'I work here,' she proffered shyly. And how glad she was that she did! How awful it would have been to be flying home with her father *now*! She caught up her thoughts, the colour running up her cheeks, and she averted her face from his bright blue eyes.

'What do you do?' he enquired. 'You must have a very easy employer, to be free at this hour.'

'It's a special occasion. Until today I worked for my father, but he's going back to England today, or rather tomorrow. He's flying up to Tehran this evening.'

'I see. And you're staying on?'

She nodded. 'The work he was doing isn't—finished.

I'm going to stay on with the new man. I've been here from the beginning of the contract.'

'A very valuable person,' he congratulated her. 'I could do with my predecessor's secretary in my job. I'm coming in right in the middle of things. It's my speciality, you might say, clearing up the mess other men leave behind them. I don't like staying anywhere too long, and that, coupled with a determination not to get involved locally, helps to put most of our less efficient projects back on their feet.'

'I've always heard Americans are ruthless business men,' she observed. 'You are American, aren't you?'

'We believe in getting things done,' he answered. 'I'm Casimir Ruddock. Most people call me Cas.'

The Ruddock part had a familiar sound, but Casimir made him seem something strange and exotic. *Casimir!* What kind of a name was that?

'My name is Stephanie Black,' she told him.

He picked up her left hand in his. '*Miss* Stephanie Black,' he said with obvious satisfaction. 'Well, Miss Stephanie Black, how about having dinner with me this evening and showing me the sights of the city? Would you have time after you've seen your father off?'

'Tonight?' she repeated. 'I have to move into my new apartment—' She broke off, staring up at him with wide eyes. 'Yes, please, I'd like to. I'd like to very much.'

'Right,' he said. He gave her an amused look. 'Was it such a difficult decision to make?'

'In a way,' she acknowledged. She didn't want him to know how inexperienced she was at allowing herself to be picked up by strangers. He was the kind of man who knew many women and he wouldn't have any time at all for the insecure, the gauche, or those who couldn't look after themselves.

'Am I such a bad risk?' he pressed her.

'I don't know.' She looked about her. 'I've never known a Casimir before!'

'Don't hold it against me,' he smiled at her. 'I come from Polish stock on my mother's side.'

Stephanie herself was English through and through. 'Oh,' she said.

'Does it put me outside the pale?'

She blinked. How could he think that? Belatedly, she realised he was teasing her and that he knew very well how she was feeling. She made a studied effort to retrieve the situation. 'Why should it?' she said. 'I'm fairly broad-minded.'

He laughed. 'I'll remember that!'

She took a step away from him, feeling dwarfed by his great height. 'I ought to be getting back to my father,' she tried to assert herself. 'I've stayed out for longer than I intended.'

He put a friendly arm round her waist and a fountain of joy began to play inside her that he had no intention of letting her go so easily. It was delightful to think that he could hold her beside him with such a minimum of effort. She doubted if he would even feel her attempt to break free—if she were to make one, and she didn't think she would. Not yet, at any rate.

'I usually pack for him,' she explained in a rush. 'Neither of my parents is much good at that sort of thing. I'm the domesticated one in the family.'

'You're too pretty for that!'

She smiled. 'Pretty? You must be prejudiced in favour of—'

'Honey-coloured blondes? I never thought about it before.' He considered the matter carefully, smiling down at her. 'I've always had pretty catholic tastes when it comes to the fair sex, but you'll do for me. Indeed you will!'

She didn't know how to answer that. It would have been trite to remind him that he didn't know anything about her. She knew nothing about him either, but she wanted to. She wanted it more badly than she had wanted anything for ages.

'But I'm not pretty,' she told him.

'Aren't you?' He was quite definitely amused now. 'Beauty lies in the eye of the beholder. Haven't you ever heard that?'

'But one *knows* about things like that,' she stammered. 'I'd know if I were pretty!'

'If you say so.' He hugged her closer to him. 'I'll see you home if you really have to go, then I'll know where to pick you up later on. But first, how do you feel about acting as my photographic model for a few minutes? The sun's just right now for a view of the domes at this end of the Maidan and I want a figure in the foreground. Will you stand over there?'

'Me?' She was enormously flattered. 'You won't really be able to see me, will you? Not if you stand far enough away to get in the whole of the outside of the mosque.'

'I'll know it's you,' he said.

She did exactly as he told her, standing in the portal of the mosque and looking up at the splendid tile-mosaics that side of the doorway. Each colour had been fired separately for the exact length of time that suited it best and made to fit the next-door piece until the whole intricate pattern was complete. It was a lengthy process, too lengthy for the impatient Shah Abbas who had ordered the mosque to be built, and on the other side of the portal the *haft-rangi* ('seven-colour') tiles had been used to speed up the work. These tiles were square and made up of several colours which were all fired at the same time. They served their purpose of covering the walls with colour quickly and economically, but they lacked the brilliance of the mosaic and their colours had faded a little over the years, not enough to matter, but enough to be noticed by a discerning eye.

'Are you ready?' Cas Ruddock asked her.

He was closer than she had expected and his camera was one of the most impressive she had ever seen, with more dials and changes of lens than she would ever have been able to cope with. She smiled across the space between them and he held up his hand to signal her to stand still and began to take a series of about a dozen photos almost before she had time to draw breath.

'Now, we'd better see about getting you home,' he said. 'Can we get a taxi from here?'

'Yes, but the buses are more fun. They stop almost outside where I live and they only cost two *rials*. You have to buy the tickets before you get on from one of those little grey kiosks. Do you mind?'

'Not if that's the way you want to travel.' He glanced at his watch. 'I'll see you home and pick you up again at about seven-thirty. Will that do you? I have a yen to see the inside of the mosque today. I guess it must be one of

15

the best known buildings in the world and once I've started work I won't have as much time as I'd like to see the sights.'

Now that the moment had come, she didn't want to leave either. If he wanted to see the mosque, why shouldn't she go inside with him? Her father wasn't expecting her back yet, though she would have to be back in time to see him off at the airport. Meanwhile, why shouldn't she enjoy herself while she could?

'I'd like to see it too,' she murmured. She stole a look at him and looked hastily away again from the amused admiration in his eyes. Was it possible that he really did find her pretty?

'Now?' he mocked her.

She was tongue-tied in the face of his assured acceptance of the fact that she would much rather be with him than packing for her father. He saw too much, she thought. If she weren't careful he would know about the fountain of joy he had inspired within her, a sensation that was still too new for her to do anything about but wonder at. He might have guessed at it already, but she didn't think he had. She stiffened her backbone and managed a quick, light smile.

'Why not now?'

'Why not indeed! Your father will have to make the best of his own ham-fisted efforts to get everything into his grip!'

And a fine mess he'd make of it, but somehow Stephanie found she didn't care as much as she should. She didn't even feel a trace of guilt at the thought of him struggling alone with his possessions. He had said he wanted it that way and although she hadn't believed him at the time, why should he have said it if he hadn't meant it?

It was fun showing the mosque to Cas Ruddock. He listened to everything she told him with a concentration that made her think she was a better guide than she had previously known. She pointed out the relief of heraldic peacocks above the central door; the two minarets, both a hundred and ten feet high; the pool, the colours of which echoed the surrounding tiles; and the great doors themselves which Shah Safi had had covered with beautifully fashioned silver plates.

Then, inside the mosque itself, passing through the half-right turn that led into the courtyard and was made necessary so that the alignment of the court and the *mihrab* pointed towards Mecca, the direction which all faithful Moslems face when they make their prayer five times each day, she allowed him to digest the beauty of the court in silence for a few minutes.

'It's typical of the Persian four-*iwan* mosque,' she told him when he seemed ready to go on. 'An *iwan* is one of those open-sided, semi-domed verandah things. It isn't a very good description, but you can see them for yourself. And look, if you stand here, you can see the huge turquoise dome that you can see when you first come into Isfahan. It's a symbol of the whole city—the glory of the Safavid monarchs who dominated the building of the city. Shah Abbas was the one who really built Isfahan and made it what it is. But the best mosque of them all, much more exciting than this one, is the Friday Mosque, and he had nothing to do with it at all. It's one of the most glorious buildings I've ever seen!'

He smiled at her enthusiasm. 'I'll get you to take me there one day—when I've found out the worst about how late we are delivering the goods on this contract. Telecommunications are the very devil to put straight when they've been allowed to get out of hand.'

Stephanie felt as though the ground had gone soft beneath her feet. 'But it's a British company that won the telecommunications contract,' she said.

'We're an international company. The British division is doing most of the work out here because we're using two of the most modern British techniques in our installations. We're using their inter-city land cables that can carry eight hundred and twenty-five circuits and more, and also trying out the Post Office fifty millimetre diameter copper waveguide. But I don't want to bore you with my work. What does your father do?'

'Telecommunications.'

'I see.' He could hardly help but see it all, she thought. He had to know exactly why her father was at that very moment packing his bags and going back to England. He probably knew more about it than she did herself. Would he like her less because of it? He shrugged his shoulders. 'Well, I don't start work until tomorrow, so we'll leave it till then, shall we?'

'Can we?' she said doubtfully.

He didn't pretend not to know what she meant. "I think so. Unless I mistake the situation from tomorrow onwards you are going to be my secretary, as you were your father's before me, but for today you're just a girl I met in Isfahan and I'm no more than someone who's determined to make you notice him in the short time he has at his disposal.'

'Yes, but tomorrow, it won't be easy for either of us, will it? I should tell you that I've never worked for anyone besides my father. You may expect too much from me.'

'Are you such a bad secretary?' he asked her.

She threaded her fingers together. 'I don't know,' she said.

'But you think my standards may be higher than your father's? Well, without wishing to offend you, my dear, you're very probably right. If you don't come up to what I expect from my secretary I shall have no hesitation in replacing you. There are other people in the company for whom you can work without having to go back to England immediately. But I'd rather worry about that tomorrow, if you don't mind? Who knows, you might be better than you think!'

The most pressing problem for her was what he wanted from her now. She looked him straight in the face, unaware that her uncertainty was written clearly in her wide hazel eyes.

'Do you still want to take me out to dinner?' she demanded. 'If I'm going to be your secretary you may not want to know me socially as well. I shall quite understand if you'd rather not.'

'I'm not a snob, Stephanie Black,' he warned her.

'No. But you're not to know that I won't take advantage—'

'Will you?'

'I'll try not to.' Her eyes flickered over his large frame and she tried to imagine herself doing the same things for him she had done for her father, and she knew then and there that it wouldn't work. 'I'd rather work for some-body else,' she said.

'We'll see,' he said comfortably. 'I don't eat my secretaries for breakfast, not unless they provoke me unbearably. Nobody who's worked for me has ever accused me of being the tyrant you seem to be afraid I'll turn out to be.'

Stephanie managed a dignified gesture of disapproval. 'It isn't that! I think I might manage the work, only when we're not working, what then? With my father it was different. I looked after him in the office and I looked after him at home and the two roles ran into each other—'

'I'm not your father,' he drawled.

He didn't have to tell her that! 'Wouldn't you find it confusing?' she murmured.

'Not in the least!' he assured her, an edge to his voice. 'As far as I'm concerned my secretary will be one person called Miss Black. Any time I spend with Stephanie will be with quite a different person, and Miss Black would be very ill advised to mention my relationship with her, or with any other of my girl-friends. Is that clear?'

'I suppose so.' She didn't like the thought that he might have other girl-friends to amuse him when he wasn't working. 'It sounds a bit cold-blooded to me. You may be big enough to be two people, but I'm sure I'll get you muddled up sooner or later!' She cast him a swift glance to see how he was taking that, hoping he hadn't noticed that she had taken his continued interest in Stephanie Black rather for granted. 'I'll try to be an ade-quate secretary,' she went on hastily, 'if you'll just be a bit patient at first. I haven't had much to do since we came here. I'm rather out of practice.'

He smiled at her and she was quite dazzled by the ironic amusement in his eyes. 'In which capacity are you asking me to be most tolerant?'

She swallowed. 'I don't know what you're talking about!' she denied crossly.

'No?' He raised an eyebrow, putting a friendly hand on her shoulder. 'I have to admit I prefer Stephanie to Miss Black,' he confessed. 'Is that what you wanted to know?'

She muttered something completely incomprehensible,

a little scared by the pleasure his words had given her.

'I think I prefer Cas too,' she mumbled under her breath. 'At least—'

His laughter brought the colour racing up her cheeks. 'Oh, don't go and spoil it!' he begged her. He touched her lips with his fingers, daring her to withdraw her preference. 'Come on, honey-child, it's time I took you home to say goodbye to your father!'

CHAPTER II

The evening wasn't at all as she had expected it to be. It seemed that Stephanie had barely recovered from the rush of seeing her father off when Cas Ruddock was at the door, smiling and assured as he dwarfed the living room which her father and she had made their own in the last few weeks.

'Was it a tough parting?' he asked her.

'So-so. I hope he finds things all right at home. I've never seen him really depressed before.' She sighed heavily. 'I can't help thinking that there's more to it than he's told me.' She turned to the large man beside her. 'Do *you* know exactly what happened?'

'More or less,' he answered.

'Then tell me!'

'Not tonight. What I need is a drink, honey—' He stressed the word slightly, knowing that she was inclined to take it personally as a reference to the colour of her hair and the honey-coloured tan her skin had gained in the Persian sun—'with ice, if you have it?'

She poured him a vodka and tonic, piling in the ice with a generous hand. 'I'm sorry it isn't whisky, but it's too expensive here. Will this do?'

'Thank you.' He accepted the glass from her hand and toasted her silently, taking a deep sip of the sparkling fluid. 'Mmm, it's not bad. How about you? You look as though you could do with something.'

Stephanie shook her head. 'A glass of wine is about my limit.' She tried to dismiss the image of her father from her mind, but the picture of his harassed expression and drooping shoulders refused to go away. Why, she wondered for the umpteenth time, had he made her stay behind?

'No head for it?' Cas teased her.

'It isn't that,' she explained, her mind obviously somewhere else. 'No taste for it!'

'I gather,' Cas observed dryly, 'that you had quite a hassle at the airport. Want to tell me about it?'

She brushed the tears out of her eyes with her fingers. 'He looked old! And he wouldn't listen to anything!

But it wouldn't be fair to talk to you about it, would it? It wouldn't be fair to him!'

'It depends whom you're telling, Cas, or Mr. Ruddock. I won't hold anything you tell me here against either your father or yourself.'

Stephanie sat down, eyeing him ruefully. 'Don't be silly,' she said. 'You may be able to play silly games about having two separate identities, but I can't! I know who you are. You're the man who's replaced my father out here, and there isn't anything you could say that would make me forget that!'

To her disappointment, Cas merely shrugged his shoulders. 'If that's the way you want it. I shan't force your confidence against your will. I can probably guess most of it anyway.'

She wondered if he could. Of one thing she was quite certain: her father had more on his mind than being recalled to England because he had failed to make a go of things in Iran. But, if he was in trouble, why had he insisted that she should stay behind and work for his successor?

'They haven't sacked him, have they?'

His blue eyes looked straight at her and she moved uncomfortably beneath their regard. He saw too much, she thought, and she didn't want him to know how much she would have liked to have turned the whole problem over to him and let him settle the whole thing for her, telling her what to do for the best.

'Not as far as I know,' he said.

'And you would know, wouldn't you?'

'I guess so.'

She bit her lip. 'Perhaps he's worried about Mother. He didn't like leaving her on her own to come out here, but her work didn't allow her to come with us. She doesn't look after herself properly half the time.'

'What does she do?' he asked her.

'She's a musician. She plays the violin a bit, and composes a bit—mostly signature tunes and background music for the television, things like that.'

'She must be an unusual lady,' Cas commented.

'She is,' Stephanie agreed, without much enthusiasm. 'The trouble is she gets carried away with some new effect and forgets everything else for hours together, Father included. I only hope she remembers to meet him at Heathrow tomorrow.'

'It must be a nice gift if you have it. Don't you like her music?'

He was far too acute! Stephanie smiled reluctantly. 'Some of it. I enjoyed her Indian phase, full of sitars and quarter-tones, but I don't like computerised music much. It's too soulless. All we had for weeks was screaming mechanical sounds while she tried them all out. After a while I could hear them clearly in the marrow of my bones and I didn't like that at all!'

Cas grinned. 'And what are your talents, Miss Stephanie Black?'

She shook her head at him. 'I haven't any—unless you count a gift for housekeeping as a talent?'

'What about your work?'

She made a face at him. 'You'll see for yourself. Most of the time I'd sooner be doing something else, though.' Her thoughts returned to her father. 'That's why I can't understand why he's gone home alone. They'll never be able to cope with getting meals and so on on their own!'

He laughed at her, swallowing the last of his drink. 'You sound as though your maternal feelings are badly outraged. I thought you were the daughter in the house!'

She flushed. 'That's what he said. He said they needed to stand on their own feet.'

'But you don't like it?' Cas accused her.

'I like to have things nice,' she excused herself. 'Neither of them ever notice when things get in a mess. They need someone to clean up after them all the time!'

'But not you,' he said with quiet certainty. 'They can hire someone if things get too bad, and they probably will. You need a man of your own to cook for and clean up after—'

'I want more out of marriage than that!' she exclaimed.

His eyes glinted dangerously. 'So will the man you marry,' he said quietly. 'Most men worth their salt don't want their emotions neatly tidied out of the way with the trash. People come before houses in my book. I never settle anywhere for long and my wife will have to pack and follow me wherever I go. It won't do either of us

23

much good if she's too busy plumping up the cushions!'

'If she's a good housekeeper she may be a good packer too,' Stephanie put in.

His eyes crinkled with amusement. 'Are you?'

'Yes,' she said, 'as a matter of fact I am.'

'I'll remember that!' He stood up, glancing round the room. 'Do you mind that I'm taking over this apartment from you?'

'Of course not!' She was glad to be able to assure him of that. 'I'll leave it all ready for you,' she promised. 'Shall I stock up the refrigerator for you?'

'No,' he snapped. 'You'll leave well alone. The last thing I want is for you to start mothering me! I'm used to doing for myself.'

She was hurt that he should be angry when she had only been trying to help. 'Then I won't remind you that you've just had most of the ice and that you'll need to make some more?' she asked him sweetly.

'No, please don't. If I don't get around to it, I'll do without. Satisfied?'

'If you are,' she said.

He reached out a long arm and hooked her neatly into the circle of his arms. 'I plan to make you an expert in something much more exciting than housewifery,' he told her. 'It's time you tried your hand at something more adventurous than your parents' washing-up!'

'I don't know what you're talking about,' she denied.

He bent his head, running his nose down the length of hers and putting his lips very gently to hers. 'Don't you?' he muttered.

It was the most unbearably exciting thing that had ever happened to her. She opened her eyes wide with shock and stepped quickly away from him. 'I thought we were going out to dinner,' she said, making a determined effort to breathe naturally and not as though she had just sprinted up four flights of stairs. 'Hadn't we better be going?'

He picked up her wrap from the back of the sofa and put it round her shoulders, carefully arranging it to his complete satisfaction. 'Don't look so frightened,' he said. 'I shan't make love to you until I've fed you—and maybe not then, unless you look a little bit more sure of yourself.

Okay?'

She nodded, feeling more than a little foolish. She cast him a speculative glance, wondering what it would be like to be kissed properly by him. She thought she might like it very much. Then he raised his eyebrows at her and she averted her gaze to the embroidered motif on her wrap.

'Do you like it?' she asked. 'I made it myself.'

'Very pretty!' he drawled. 'Just like its owner!' He turned her face up to his with a masterful hand. 'Do you want me to kiss you, Stephanie?'

'Of course not!' she gasped.

'Liar! I think you're as much tempted as I am.' He fondled her cheek, letting her go with an abruptness that made her stumble over her own feet. 'We'd better go! I'm spending the night at the Shah Abbas and I thought we might eat there. I'll leave it to you what we do afterwards.'

Now what did he mean by that? Should she make it clear once and for all that she wasn't given to amorous adventures? It would be quite impossible for her to bring the subject up of her own volition, so it was now or never. She took a deep breath and rushed into agitated speech:

'Cas, I'm a very ordinary sort of person. We hardly know each other at all. Perhaps I'm more reserved because I'm English, but I don't go round kissing people on such a short acquaintance.' She felt quite weak at the knees and, rather belatedly, she became aware that she was clutching his hand as though her life depended on it. 'I'm not—'

'Very experienced?'

She nodded her head, not daring to look at him.

'My dear girl, what kind of a man do you think I am? No, don't answer that! I can guess! What do you want me to do? I can't alter the fact that I've known a great many women in my time, but I can't help thinking you wouldn't like me half so much if I were an inexperienced boy without any idea as to what he was about?'

'It isn't that!' she protested. 'It's nothing to do with you at all! Not directly anyway. It's just that I think you ought to know that I don't want to have an affair with anyone, and certainly not with my *employer*. So if that's

25

why you asked me to have dinner with you I'm not coming. I'd rather—rather not go out with you on those terms!'

'What makes you think I want to seduce you?' he demanded with a wry smile. 'Aren't you afraid of putting the idea into my head?'

'I think it was there already,' she said seriously.

'But you don't like me enough?'

She lifted her chin a little. 'It isn't a question of liking. I like you very much—what I know of you—but—oh well, let's just say I'm old-fashioned about these things.' She managed to look at him then. 'Do you mind?'

'No, I don't think I do.' His eyes were bright with amusement and with something else that set her heart beating like a mad thing within her. 'I can wait!'

She was inclined to be indignant. 'I shan't change my mind!' she declared with a violence that betrayed to her, if not to him, that she wasn't nearly as sure of herself as she would have liked to have been.

'Circumstances may change it for you,' he retorted. 'And I? Do I have no say in the matter?'

She shook her head silently, determined to make him see that her moral values were not a whim that she held by today and forgot all about next week. *Nothing* would make her change her mind!

'We'll see!' he mocked her. 'As I said before, I can wait!'

She devoutly hoped that he was wrong. 'You'll have to wait a long, long time!' she told him.

He smiled at that. 'Not so very long,' he said, 'not for what I want. I always get what I want in the end, one way or another, and so I warn you!'

She ought to have been shocked. At the very least she ought to have been afraid that he might be right. But she was neither of those things. All she felt was a wild, exultant glow of happiness that he still meant to take her out to dinner. After all, she told herself, he wasn't to know how seldom she had been asked out by a man before, and she wasn't entirely averse to the spice of danger that he had added to the occasion. Far from it! She could have hugged herself with glee that he should actually want to kiss her!

She looked up at him and grinned, laughter lighting her eyes. 'You'll have to marry me first!' she teased him. 'And so I warn you!'

There was no answering smile on Cas's face. 'I've already thought of that,' he said.

'Isfahan is half the world,' Stephanie quoted, looking round the fabulously ornate dining room of the Shah Abbas Hotel.

Cas nodded. 'I suspect there's been some European influence brought to bear here, though,' he remarked. 'It's too symmetrical—too perfect to be wholly Persian.'

Stephanie eyed him across the table, liking him very much. 'You'll love the Friday Mosque,' she told him. 'There must be hundreds of arches there, all the same, but all a little bit different. I defy anyone to get bored with looking at it. One day we must go there.'

'We will!'

Something in his tone of voice reminded her of their final exchange in the apartment. She had been trying not to think about it because it did funny things to her inside, almost as though she were housing a wild animal in there. She felt very strange and not at all like herself.

'They say,' she said with a touch of desperation, 'that Isfahan is the meaning of the world; "World" is the word and "Isfahan" the meaning.'

'Who says?'

'I don't know,' she admitted. 'I read it somewhere.'

She abandoned her attempt to make conversation after that. She allowed her eyes to wander over the decorated panels that decorated the walls of the room, and upwards to the balcony overhead. Persian paintings fascinated her at the best of times, especially the older ones. Strongly influenced by both China and India, or was it the other way round, they obeyed few of the known rules of perspective, and yet were easy to interpret, the horses thundering over the ground, the carpet canopies swaying with motion, and the rich and successful easy to tell from the poor and captive.

Most of the dishes on the menu were of the usual international kind, but Stephanie was delighted to see one or two which were really Persian and after some consideration chose to have a basis of rice with chicken and a pomegranate sauce. She had already discovered that the long, curly-grained Iranian rice was one of the most delicious varieties she had ever eaten, and she was curious to discover if their sauces, which she knew they favoured eating with huge piles of rice, were equally good.

When she had finished her discussion with the waiter, she was embarrassed to find that Cas had been watching her throughout the time it had taken to make up her mind and she wondered if he resented her speaking directly to the waiter without waiting to make her choice through him.

'It seems to be called *Khoreshe Fesenjan*. *Khoreshe* must mean sauce. What are you having?'

Cas smiled at the note of apology in her voice. 'I'll have the same. And a good local wine, if there is one?'

The waiter explained the Iranian system of calling all their wines by numbers, recommending a light claret type wine that was produced by the Armenians who had been brought to Persia many centuries before.

'I didn't know there were Armenians in Iran,' Cas said when the waiter had gone. 'I thought they had been dispossessed of their lands, first in Armenia itself, and then in Turkey. They haven't any homeland of their own now, have they?'

'I don't think so,' Stephanie replied. 'But they have their own church and their own customs. They're very much a distinct people still. Shah Abbas brought them to Isfahan from Julfa, which is now in the Soviet Union. They live across the river in a suburb called New Julfa, safe from persecution. The Persians have always been tolerant of other people. You remember it was Cyrus who allowed the Jews to return to the Holy Land from Babylon? And the Armenians have certainly returned the hospitality they received then and now. They are some of the best craftsmen around—and some of the most astute businessmen!'

Cas smiled slowly. 'You like it here, don't you?' he said.

'Yes, I do.' She didn't try to explain the passionate liking she had for Isfahan. It had come as a surprise to her when, after she and her father had more or less settled into the apartment the company had hired for them, she had found herself feeling more at home in this foreign city than she ever had in her parents' home in Surrey. 'Perhaps what they say is right,' she said shyly. 'Perhaps that's the meaning of the world that we find here. Beautiful buildings, paintings, tree-lined streets, and a pride in living, are better values than our technology gives us. It would be a pity if it were all to change now.'

'Don't you approve of better communications?' he asked her.

'In their place. I don't think they should be confused with civilisation—to me they're quite different!'

His eyes narrowed as he watched her closely. 'You think we can have one without the other?'

She was unused to having her ideas taken seriously and for one blank, rather frightening moment she wondered exactly what she did think about it.

'No,' she said at last. 'One has to have technology before one can have any civilisation that's worthy of the name, but technology is the servant and has to remain so if the all-important human dimension of life is to be kept. As soon as it becomes the master, mankind loses something of itself.'

'Like your mother's computed music?' he suggested.

She was glad he had understood her meaning so quickly. 'It's only my personal opinion,' she said. 'I don't expect you to agree with me, though. Technology must mean a lot to you.'

'A lot, but not everything.'

He changed the subject when their food came, amused by the careful way she tasted the dish she had chosen and smiling at her pleased expression when she found she liked it.

'What are you thinking about now?' he asked her.

'I was tasting to see what's in it,' she confessed. 'It would be nice to be able to make it myself. I like trying new, exotic dishes.' She sat back, defeated. 'It's too complicated to distinguish all the ingredients,' she said, disappointed. 'Bother!'

'Does it mean so much to you?' Cas teased her.

'I suppose it does. I find it interesting, like you do digital coding or something like that. I enjoy cooking.'

Cas flicked his fingers to the waiter and pointed to his plate. 'Find out from the chef how he made this, will you,' he ordered him. 'Miss Black wants to know. Oh, and tell him that we find it delicious, so delicious we want to be able to make it for ourselves.'

A little pink, Stephanie cast him a reproving look, but the waiter was all smiles as he hurried away on his mission. When he came back, he was carrying a piece of paper in his hand with the recipe written in both Persian and English which he handed to Stephanie with a triumphant flourish.

'The chef, he says you must put all these things in for the sauce to be correct,' he told her. 'Chicken, shortening, tomato sauce, onion, walnuts, cinnamon, lemon juice and, most important of all, the pomegranate juice and the seasonings. You see, he has written all the quantities you will need down the side. Good fortune when you make it for yourself and the gentleman!'

'Oh! I don't know that Mr. Ruddock—'

'I shall expect it to taste just like this,' Cas cut her off lazily, and he turned and thanked the waiter, putting a couple of bank notes into his hand for himself and the chef.

'You shouldn't have gone to so much trouble,' Stephanie reproved him.

'Why not? I'd go to just as much trouble to understand the advantages of digital coding and how it works, I assure you.'

'But that's your work! Cooking is just a hobby with me!'

He grinned. 'Is it? I'll believe that when I see you looking equally enthusiastic over typing one of my reports,' he said.

'I don't often understand them,' she said on a sigh. She blinked, hiding her eyes behind her lashes. 'I'm not looking forward to tomorrow,' she confided. 'I'm afraid you'll expect too much.'

'Don't think about it,' he advised. 'I'll give you a fair trial—I can't say fairer than that, can I?'

'No,' she admitted. 'Only I don't want to get all hurt and upset, and I know I will if I can't do what you ask!'

He smiled across the table at her. 'Women! They always take everything so darned personally. You'll have to learn to separate your work from your personal life, honey. We all have to, sooner or later.'

'But what if I can't?'

'We'll have to think of something else for you to do.' He put his hand over hers. 'Don't look like that, my dear. There's no reason why you shouldn't manage very well, is there? You must have learned something, working for your father, and I'm told I'm fairly easy to work for.'

'I hope so,' she said.

'Does it matter so much to you?'

She nodded. 'I expect it seems silly to you, but working for one's father isn't much of a test of what one can really do. I mean, he would never have told me to go—he'd more likely have got in someone to help me. I want to be a success in my own right.'

'That's up to you, my sweet. If you want it enough, I daresay you'll make your mark. But you'll have to do it on your own. I can't help you. I shall expect exactly the same from you as I would from any other girl I had working for me. It doesn't do to play favourites in an office.'

'I wouldn't ask you to,' she replied proudly. 'That's the *last* thing I'd ask! I want to do it all on my own. Father made enough of a mess without my adding to things.' She hesitated, beginning to worry again. 'It wasn't his fault! The equipment he was expecting didn't arrive and the men began to take advantage. The spring was late in coming this year and one of the teams ran into a pack of wolves. They kept one man up a post for days, threatening him every time he made to come down, and everybody thought Father should have done something about that too. But what could he have done?'

Cas didn't answer directly. 'He'll be happier back in England,' he said.

'Will he?' She was remembering her father's dejected frame as he had departed up the steps into the aeroplane. 'He won't know what to do with himself unless they find him a proper job to do, and it's so long since he had to tackle anything by himself.'

'He has your mother to support him,' Cas pointed out

31

with a cheerfulness that Stephanie thought was quite uncalled for. 'He doesn't need you to hold his hand as well.' He gave her hand a sharp tap before taking back his own. 'You have your own problems to worry about! When you've finished your coffee, we'll go for a stroll down by the river and look at the bridges I've heard so much about. You'll have your hands more than full to keep me from kissing you in the moonlight beside the Khajou Bridge, if it's as romantic as it looks in the picture in my bedroom.'

She looked down her nose and pretended she hadn't heard him. 'They used to dam the river there and hold water sports and spectaculars in the lake they made. But the Zayanderud is only a trickle nowadays and there's nothing to dam. Farmers have planted crops in the river bed and they sometimes even play football there. One day they may dam the river again, but it will be near the Shahrestan Bridge if they do.'

'Is the Khajou the best of the Safavid bridges?' Cas encouraged her.

'I think so. I think it's one of the most impressive of the Safavid monuments. But you'll see it for yourself. It's hard to believe it was built as long ago as 1660.' She felt a great deal safer discussing the bridge and went on to tell him about the two tiers of arches which spanned the river; forty-eight on the upper tier and twenty-four on the lower. In the middle is a hexagonal pavilion, with two mosaic-decorated *iwans* facing outwards. In the days when people had picnicked in the arches, worshipped in the chapel, and bought and sold their goods under the arches, the bridge must have been a hive of industry. It was still incredibly, heart-stoppingly beautiful.

'I look forward to our visit,' Cas said, his eyes snapping with laughter. 'It sounds every bit as romantic as I had hoped!'

Well, so it was, but Stephanie didn't know that she wanted to accompany him there. 'How will we get there?' she asked. 'It's too far to walk.'

'We'll do it properly and go in the hotel's horse-drawn carriage,' he retorted, unperturbed. 'Shall we go?'

It was silly to be afraid and she refused to be anything so lacking in spirit. But she took the precaution of sitting

32

as far away from him as she could in the carriage, taking a deep interest in the crowded streets they passed through, a little annoyed that he wasn't in the least put out by her cautious attitude.

Indeed, he hardly touched her fingers as he helped her down to the ground when they arrived at the bridge and he dismissed her with a lack of interest that was very nearly insulting as he walked as close to the bridge as he could get, his hands in his pockets, apparently completely absorbed in the ancient bridge.

She walked after him, plucking at the sleeve of his coat. 'Look,' she pointed out, 'you can see the twenty-four slabs of masonry on which the whole bridge stands down there. Those narrow channels formed the dam—Oh! *Cas*!' But she was too late. His hand shot out and she was lifted bodily against his huge frame, her feet several inches off the ground. 'Cas, you can't! Not here!'

She could feel his laughter and she marvelled that he could hold hold her so easily. 'Why not here?' he murmured against her lips. 'Nobody can see us in the shadow of the bridge. Don't kick, my little love. It won't make any difference and you know it. I've been wanting to do this ever since I first saw you!'

She had wanted it too. His lips ignited a flame within her and in an instant she was surrounded by a dazzling, warm delight that went off inside her like the finale of a fireworks display.

'Oh, Cas!' she whispered.

But his only answer was to kiss her all over again.

CHAPTER III

Stephanie hardly slept at all that night. If she wasn't very careful, she told herself, she would lose her sense of proportion altogether. Such a swift, unexpected embrace should not be built up into a world-shattering event, the most important thing that had ever happened to her in her whole life. So what if he had kissed her? She, and how many others?

Yet there had been a certain star-spangled splendour about the evening which refused to go away. Not even the prospect of being Miss Black and having to go to work just as though nothing had happened could quite banish the glow that surrounded her.

Cautiously, hedging her recollections about with stern reminders that she was not to make too much of them, she allowed herself to dwell once again on the silent journey they had made coming back from the bridge. Neither of them had said a single word; she, out of sheer nervousness, and he—? He wasn't the type to suffer from nerves. Besides, it couldn't have been the brand new, shattering experience for him that it had been for her. Perhaps he had been savouring his conquest, which it had been, she confessed to herself, for her defences had crumbled at his very first touch—and she *had liked it*!

So where did she go from here? When she shut her eyes she could still hear the horse's hooves and the jangle of the harness and the complete silence within the carriage itself. Why hadn't he said anything? Was it because she had disappointed him in some way? Perhaps he hadn't wanted to kiss her again? She felt a pain in her middle at the thought. How would she ever know how he had felt? Certainly not in the office while she was acting as his secretary. She would have to school herself to be as impersonal as he all the time she was working for him. but at least it would be an opportunity to get to know him better on a safe, ordinary level. And that would be a very good thing, she told herself severely. She wasn't the type to lose her head just because a man had kissed her. Well— perhaps she had lost her head, a little, but she certainly

34

wasn't going to lose anything else! Her heart would be bestowed only after she was sure that it would be properly valued by the recipient. Untidy love affairs were not for anyone who liked everything in its proper place as she did. She would have to see to it that he didn't kiss her again until she was quite, quite sure what he meant by it.

It seemed strange to push open the heavy swing door that led to the company's offices on her own. In all the time she had been working she had always arrived in her father's company. Now she was on her own and she hoped passionately that she would be able to manage with no one to turn to at the first sign of trouble. She smiled at the Iranian who looked after the reception area and was rewarded by his answering grin.

'*Salaam*, Ali,' she murmured. 'I'm not the last, I hope?'

'The new boss is not here yet,' he answered in his careful English. He answered an imperative buzz from the internal telephone at his side. 'They are asking where you are, Miss Black,' he told her. 'There is some trouble up in your office.'

Stephanie stepped into the lift, steeling herself to press the button that would take her up to her floor. Every time she did so she got a mild shock, and the sensation didn't appeal to her. In vain, she had spoken to her father about it, but he had dismissed it as a commonplace vagary of local workmanship.

'They *all* do it, Stephanie,' he had told her wearily. 'It's just the same when I open my window in the office. You'll get used to it.'

The lift staggered upward, came to a halt between floors, the lights flickering uncertainly, and then reversed itself and went back down to the ground floor again. Stephanie sighed with irritated resignation. That was another thing that it would take her time to get used to. She liked lifts to arrive at their first destination *before* rushing off to obey the next summons.

The doors swished open and Cas looked at her in surprise.

'I thought only children played at going up and down in elevators, Miss Black?'

She cast him a speaking look. 'Good morning, Mr.

35

Ruddock,' she said with visible restraint.

Cas eased himself into the small space beside her and she kindly allowed him to get the electric shock by pressing the button this time.

'Just as well I haven't got a tin arm,' he commented. 'Have this fault seen to, will you, Miss Black?'

'You get used to it,' she answered, just as her father had done. 'My father said the window in his—your office—'

'Get it seen to,' he cut her off.

'It will take time to get an engineer,' she warned him.

'Don't be silly, Miss Black. The whole place is bulging with engineers. If you can't get in a local electrician, you'd better make up to one of our own men and see what he can do. I dislike being surrounded by things that don't work properly.'

He could say that again as far as people were concerned too, his tone of voice informed her, and she gritted her teeth. It was obviously useless to point out the impossibility of trying to change something that was considered normal by everyone else.

'I'll try,' she muttered.

'If you're wise,' he retorted, 'you'll get it done!'

Quite why it should annoy her that this time the lift should arrive at the right floor without incident, Stephanie could not have said. That it did, she found very hard to hide as she stepped out of the lift before Cas, taking a deep breath to celebrate the sudden freedom from being crowded by his huge frame in such a restricted space. It was that which had made breathing difficult inside the lift, of course. She had had no trouble in that direction before he had got in.

The knot of girls standing in the doorway of her office made her pause. She had always got on fairly well with them all, but she was wise enough to know that there had been a certain restraint between herself and them. They had never forgotten that the man she worked for was not only the head of the Iranian project but her father as well. It had been natural that they should have been careful of what they said to her and had avoided being seen to be too friendly with her.

Fatemeh, the most senior of the Iranian girls, turned and saw her first. 'It is terrible! Who could have done this thing!' she burst out, the tears pouring down her face. She changed to her own language in a flood of speech that became more and more hysterical.

'Please, Fatemeh, I don't understand a single word you're saying—'

The Persian girl fell back against the wall. 'Look!' The stark tragedy in her tones aroused an urge in Stephanie to giggle which she suppressed with some difficulty. 'See for yourself!'

Stephanie peered over another girl's shoulder into her own office and was astonished to see papers everywhere, scattered all over the floor, pulled at random out of files, and left in tottering piles all over her desk.

The only other English secretary, a girl called Gloria, pointed faintly into the room with her nail file. 'Did you ever see anything like it?'

'But why?' Stephanie gasped.

'And who?' Gloria added. 'I'd like to know who even more. Who else has the keys to your files, love?'

Stephanie went pale. 'No one,' she murmured.

'Not your father?' Gloria insisted.

Stephanie shook her head. 'I have his keys too.'

'Oh yes, I'd forgotten. He's gone back to England, hasn't he? Have you seen the new man yet? It'll be quite a change for you, won't it? And what will he say about this?'

Stephanie had no idea. She pushed through the cluster of people in the doorway and stood in the middle of her office, looking gloomily about her. Was that why her father had looked so bent and defeated as he had flown off the day before? Had *he* had something to do with this? Stephanie would not allow herself even to consider such a thing. Her father was entitled to her loyalty and she had always given it to him unstintingly, and now was the time when he needed it most of all, when he had been recalled England and his job given to another. Why would he need the papers anyway? If he had asked her, she would have made him a parting present of the lot of them!

'Will you know if anything is missing?' Fatemeh enquired. 'I can send some girls up to help you put things straight, if you wish me to?'

'Thank you,' Stephanie returned automatically, 'but

I'd better do it myself. A lot of the papers are confidential—' She broke off, feeling quite hollow inside. The confidential papers had been mostly to do with the equipment they were still waiting for and the resulting letters between her father and the head office in London. They weren't letters that she relished falling into anyone else's hands. Her father's letters had begun by being querulous and had ended on a whining note that she had regretted and had done her best to soften by changing a word here and there as she had typed them. The replies had been as bad. They had given him a free hand to do his own bargaining from the very beginning, until at last, patience exhausted, they had sent a terse message recalling him to London and appointing someone else in his place.

Cas Ruddock! Stephanie blinked, hoping against hope that he wouldn't need her for anything in the next couple of hours. He was the very last person she wanted to see those letters—or to know if any of them were missing.

'Fatemeh, I've changed my mind. I'd like some help if you can spare someone for an hour or so. I can sort and she can put away. The sooner we get this mess cleared out of the way the better!'

Gloria tapped Stephanie's arm with her nail file. 'If you take my advice, you'll take time out to confess all to the new boss,' she advised without malice. 'He'll have to know in the end and you don't want him to go thinking things you'd rather he didn't, do you?'

'Like what?' Stephanie demanded.

'Like you have the keys and could be hiding something up for your father,' Gloria drawled.

Stephanie looked paler than ever. 'You don't think that, do you?' she almost pleaded.

'No, I don't,' Gloria maintained. 'But what I think doesn't matter. If you ask me, you'd have been far too busy packing your father's bags and fretting over his departure for you to have had time to come back here. But who else could it have been?'

Her father himself? 'I don't know,' Stephanie admitted She examined the drawers of the file which was always kept locked and, with a sinking heart, noticed they

38

hadn't been forced or broken into. 'Someone else must have a set of keys.'

'A likely tale!' Gloria murmured.

The sudden silence amongst the girls in the doorway made Stephanie turn her head to see what was happening, but she knew, even before she saw him, that it was Cas who had caused the flutter and the ensuing quiet. The girls were looking at him as though they had never seen a man before, and Gloria was the worst of them all, fluttering her eyelashes and smiling like the cat who had just swallowed the pet canary.

'Stephanie,' she whispered, 'who's *this*?'

'Mr. Ruddock,' Stephanie's voice didn't sound like her own and she cleared her throat with a nervous smile of her own. 'My—my father's replacement,' she added unnecessarily.

'But you're an American!' Gloria exclaimed. 'How interesting!'

'Fascinating,' Cas drawled. 'What's been going on here?'

'Oh, Mr. Ruddock, we don't know! We found it like this! Isn't it awful?'

Cas almost smiled at her. 'If you say so, Miss—?'

'Gloria.'

'Gloria what?' he demanded, his irritation, getting the better of him. 'I think you should know that I think it a mistake to introduce first names into one's place of work. It leads to slackness in other areas all too easily.'

'But I thought Americans—' Gloria began, changed her mind and tried another smile. 'Lake,' she supplied reluctantly. 'Gloria Lake. My mother was going to call me Veronica, but my father didn't like the idea. Pity, isn't it?'

Cas looked baffled. 'Veronica Lake was a film star,' Stephanie supplied, struggling not to laugh.

Cas turned to her with something like relief. 'Have you seen about that lift yet?' he barked at her.

She was justifiably incensed. 'The lift? I haven't given it another thought! I can't do everything at once!'

'Forgive me, but it doesn't look as though any of you are doing anything!' he shot back. 'What is all this anyway?'

39

Fortunately for her peace of mind, Stephanie didn't know how frightened she looked. 'Someone must have broken in—'

'Has anything been taken?'

'I don't think so,' she managed to say. 'They've had all the files out, though. Some of them are rather confidential and we've always kept them locked.' She stood her ground, looking him straight in the eyes. 'I have the only keys. My father gave me his set yesterday *morning*.' She thought that by stressing the word she had made things worse than they were. 'I mean, I locked them up myself and I had all the keys in my possession then. The files haven't been forced. I don't understand it!'

With a single look he sent the girls running back to work and even Gloria and Fatemeh began to gather themselves up as though they meant to go and do some work, albeit rather reluctantly.

Cas shut the door with a snap, almost catching their skirts in it in his hurry.

'Now, Miss Black, tell me all about it,' he invited her.

'I can't understand it!' she repeated.

'It would seem pretty obvious that someone else has a set of keys,' he said.

'But they haven't!'

'You're sure of that?'

She nodded helplessly. 'I made sure of it because— well, because the interchange between my father and our head office was best not seen by too many others. The other confidential files are the records of all employees working in Iran and other things like that. Nothing that would be of any use to anyone outside the firm.'

'But it might be useful to someone inside the company?'

'It could be,' she admitted. 'We only just managed to get this contract and the delays haven't helped us. The exact state of play would be of interest to any of our competitors. We could even lose the contract if we fall down on any of the terms of the agreement.'

'You're telling me!' His tone was wry, but not unreasonable. 'You think that's the most likely explanation, Stephanie?'

'Yes.' She flushed, moving a pile of papers on her desk from one place to another. 'No. My father could have taken my keys yesterday afternoon when I was out.' She gave him a shy look, remembering vividly their meeting in the Maidan. 'I left them on my bedside table. I picked them up there this morning.'

'It would be one way of getting his own back on the company,' Cas said slowly. 'I wouldn't have thought it of a man like Desmond Black, however. You'd better get someone else to clear up in here. I want you with me this morning.' He put out a hand and lifted her chin with a single finger. 'Don't look like that, my dear. We'll get to the bottom of it sooner or later, I promise you that.'

'I may not want to know,' she whispered.

'That's a risk you'll have to take.' He looked at her, a smile gleaming in the back of his eyes. 'By the way, how popular are you with your colleagues?'

'I get on with them all right.' She escaped his touch with a jerk of her head. 'They wouldn't have done this because of me!'

'I hope not.' He said it quietly, almost like a prayer, and she shivered, wondering if she could possibly have inspired that much hate amongst the people she worked with. It was no better than the alternative that her father had done this to conceal some letter from his successor's and perhaps her own eyes.

'Fatemeh is sending up someone to help restore order, but I shall have to do most of it myself,' she began to explain the obvious to him in an attempt to escape the implications of her thoughts. 'Some of the files are confidential.'

He grinned at her. 'You're itching to get your fingers on that mess, aren't you? It offends you to see everything upside down like that, doesn't it?'

'I suppose it does,' she admitted.

'Poor Stephanie! At least I can be pretty sure that you didn't do it! If you had, you'd have left everything as neat as ever, wouldn't you?'

'Would I?' She opened her eyes wide, a little surprised at herself.

'Of course you would! Do you really have to put it to rights straight away? I want you beside me when I make my presence felt this morning. Lock your door and leave it until later.'

'Until this afternoon?' she mused. 'I could do that, I suppose.'

'If you have to go on after hours I'll come and give you a hand,' he offered. 'Will that suit you?'

It was ridiculous to feel so happy at the prospect, but she couldn't hide the fact that she liked being with him, no matter what the circumstances. 'I expect I'll have finished before then,' she said soberly. 'One thing is certain, I can't do any work in that room until I have got it back in order!'

He looked amused. 'Come along then, Miss Black. We'd better go and face life in my office where there's no mess to offend you. Will you lock the door, or shall I?'

There followed a morning that was quite different from any that Stephanie had spent working for her father. Where her father had hesitated, compromised, and delayed making any final decision until he had had time to think through the matter, Cas was quick to evaluate any problem and snapped out the solution he had decided on, passing on to the next item almost before she was aware. By lunchtime they had completed as much work as she usually did in a month and she felt as though a steamroller had passed right over her.

'Right,' Cas said at last. 'That seems to be all for now. I shan't expect those letters until tomorrow, but normally I like to sign everything before I go home at night. You'd better go and have some lunch now, Miss Black.'

'Thank you,' she said.

He tipped his chair back on to two legs, watching her through half-closed eyes. She wished he wouldn't. She was sure the chair would collapse under his weight and she didn't like being looked at in that way, just as though she had a smut on her nose! She passed a harassed hand through her hair and wondered why that seemed to amuse him. She took a quick step away from him when he stood up, but she hadn't a hope of escaping his long arm.

'Why are you in such a tizzy?' he grinned at her. He rucked up her hair, making it stand on end, with the pleased look of a small boy. 'It does you good to get mussed up once in a while. What are you doing for lunch?

She smoothed down her hair with an indignant hand,

making good her escape as fast as she could. But when she shut the door behind her, she could hear him laughing at her and she found she was smiling herself. What a strange man he was! One moment working with a speed and precision that bore witness to his dedication and the next as playful as a child without a care in the world!

'Oh, Stephanie, I *like* your hair like that!' Gloria ran down the passage, catching up with her. 'A half-fringe really suits you! When did you decide to have it done like that?'

They disappeared into the cloakroom together and Stephanie made a little rush towards the nearest looking-glass before she had to answer the other English girl.

'I *like* it!' she exclaimed, marvelling at her reflection.

'Why not?' Gloria shrugged. 'It makes you look softer, more approachable. I suppose you feel you can relax a bit now that it isn't your father you're working for. You always looked so severe and devoted to the cause! If I'd been you, I'd have chucked it long ago! I like to live my own life.'

But if she kept it, would Cas recognise what he had inadvertently created? Would he even notice? She touched the fringe he had given her with tentative fingers, pushing it into a better shape.

'I like it!' she declared again.

'Good for you,' Gloria retorted, rapidly losing interest. 'Talking about living you own life, where are you living now? I suppose the big man wanted your father's apartment for himself?'

Stephanie nodded. 'I have a smaller place in the same building—just a room really, but it's quite nice.'

Gloria turned speculative eyes on to her. 'Bit of a change for you all the same. You'll notice the difference when you have to pay for everything yourself. I thought when we first arrived it would be fun having another English girl around, but you believe in keeping yourself to yourself, don't you? Shall we see more of you now that you haven't got Daddy to run home to every evening?'

'Possibly.'

'Well, I wish you would!' Gloria went on. 'There's not much a girl can do on her own here. The Persian girls have their mothers after them if they so much as smile at a man on their way home, and their families have hysterics if they're half an hour late, or anything like that. I've been downright lonely since I've been here.'

'Oh, Gloria, I'm sorry. I never thought!' Stephanie said quickly. 'You should have said something before. You could at least have come home sometimes with Father and myself.'

'Thanks very much! That wasn't quite what I hand in mind! Now if your father had been more like Mr. Ruddock I might have considered it! Why do you suppose they chose an American to run things? I thought this was a strictly English contract! Though he's dishy enough for me whatever he is! Did you ever see such a huge man, and handsome with it?'

'I suppose he is,' Stephanie said, as if she had just discovered the fact.

'You don't mean you haven't noticed!' Gloria expostulated. 'Come to think of it, you might not have done. I suppose living with Daddy rather cramped your style where men are concerned?'

'I've never thought about it,' Stephanie answered truthfully.

'You may not have thought of it before,' Gloria observed with relish, 'but working with him every day, you'd better wake up and think about it now! What I'd give to have your opportunities!'

Stephanie thought rather less highly of her opportunities that afternoon when she unlocked the door of her office and began to take stock of the damage that had been done to her filing system. She cleared a space in the middle of the room and sat on the floor, putting the papers in neat piles all round her. Nothing seemed to be missing, but then nothing was in its right place either. It all seemed to be a completely meaningless bit of vandalism, and she would have dismissed it as such if it hadn't been for the planning that must have been involved in getting hold of the keys to the files.

Fatemeh put her head round the door quite early in the afternoon.

'I've come to help you myself,' she announced. 'There's been too much talk about this downstairs already and I don't want to encourage it. What shall I

44

do first?'

Stephanie pointed out the various piles that could be safely filed away. 'I'd rather you left the last two to me,' she said. 'I want to make absolutely sure that there's nothing missing from the confidential files.'

Fatemeh nodded. She was a pretty girl, intelligent, with a bright perky way of speaking that disguised her essentially placid good nature. It had taken a lot of persuasion for her family to allow her to work for a foreign company and she was always met at the door by one of the maids of the house who, as closely veiled in a *chador* as her young mistress, escorted her to and from her home daily.

'Do you know why it happened?' the Persian girl asked as she settled to her task. 'Has it to do with your father?'

'I don't know,' Stephanie admitted. 'If my father had wanted any of these letters, he only had to ask, or he could have got it himself. Why all this?'

Fatemeh smiled across at her. 'I like your father, which is why I haven't told anyone else, but he was here yesterday afternoon, I saw him myself.'

'You *saw* him? But what did he say?'

Fatemeh shrugged. 'I said I was sorry he was leaving and he said he was too. Naturally, I didn't ask him what he was doing in his own daughter's office.' The Persian girl lowered her eyes and blushed. 'He did say that it was all a misunderstanding that he had to go back to England, but that he would be back soon enough. He said I was a good girl and I was to look after you until he came back to Isfahan. He was afraid Mr. Ruddock got ideas about you!'

'And what are you supposed to do if he does?' Stephanie asked dryly.

'I can always be there if you need me. He is intimidating, this Mr. Ruddock, don't you think? He is so large!'

'Gloria doesn't seem to think so!'

Fatemeh laughed. 'Gloria doesn't have to work for him!' She pursed up her lips thoughtfully. 'You must not let Gloria make you do things you would rather not. She is English like yourself, but not at all the same. I would not take *her* home to meet my family.'

Touched by her obvious concern, Stephanie made a

45

small movement of protest. 'Gloria is all right. I think she's a bit lonely.'

'If she is, it is not for lack of company. She knows many men in the city, but few women. My brother knows her.'

Stephanie went on resolutely sorting out the papers in front of her. She would have liked to have asked Fatemeh what else she knew about Gloria, but she didn't think she ought to encourage her to gossip. That was the hardest part of being the boss's secretary, she was always inhibited when she was talking to the other girls in the office.

She picked up a new pile of letters and rested them on her knee, riffling through them to get them into some kind of order before she carefully checked the date of each one in turn. It was only then she realised that there were letters there that she had never seen before. Yet on each one was her father's initials followed by her own as the ostensible typist of the letter. She began to look at them more closely, putting the ones she knew nothing about in a separate pile on their own. Only when she had collected them all together did she begin to read through them, intrigued to find out what they were all about. And then she wished she hadn't. They were mainly letters her father had written to the suppliers of most of the telecommunications equipment they had been waiting for. The only difference was that in these letters the whole order had been cancelled and in terms which had called forth an irate reply and threats to sue for breach of contract.

Stephanie hid the letters under her skirt without any idea as to what she was going to do with them. She went on sorting the rest of the papers automatically and in silence, hardly acknowledging Fatemeh's delight in their progress at all.

'Are you tired, Stephanie?' the Persian girl asked her. 'Shall I go now? We can finish it tomorrow, yes?'

'Yes, good idea,' Stephanie agreed. She thanked the other girl as warmly as she could, swallowing down her relief in being left alone, and yet afraid to have no further excuse not to come to some decision about the letters she had found.

Yet when she was alone she went on sitting on the

46

floor, doing nothing at all but trying to blink back the tears that suddenly afflicted her. She didn't even notice when the door opened again and Cas came in.

'Stephanie, I told you to get something done about that lift!' He came nearer, reaching down and swinging her up on to her feet. 'What's happened now, little one? Whatever it is, it isn't worth crying over, is it? Have you got a handkerchief?' He gave her a resigned look as she shook her head. 'Of course not! What woman ever has? You'd better use mine, and then when you've dried out you can tell me all about it.'

CHAPTER IV

'Now, what's it all about?'

'Nothing,' she sobbed. 'Absolutely nothing! Nothing I can tell you about anyway. You're the last person I can tell!'

'I hadn't realised I was such an ogre!' He put his arms right round her and buried her head in his chest. Accustomed as she was to being as tall, or very nearly so, as the men she knew, it had a strange effect on Stephanie to find herself cradled like a child against him.

'Don't touch me!' she warned him. 'It makes it worse!'

But far from letting her go, he only held her the tighter, an odd smile playing round his lips. 'In what way worse?' he asked her. His hands caressed her back, tracing the line of her spine with gentle fingers.

'Don't!' she repeated.

'Why not?'

She felt quite weak at the knees, with all thought of the letters forgotten. Where were all her fine resolutions now? All she wanted was to be closer still to him, to have his lips claim hers once again, and to hold him tightly against her while he kissed her.

'I haven't finished work yet,' she said foolishly.

'Oh yes, you have, my dear! You finish when I tell you to, or are you going to make a habit of arguing with your boss? I shouldn't advise it. I have ways of dealing with recalcitrant secretaries.'

'Have you?' She couldn't think of anything he might do that she wouldn't welcome with open arms. She gave him a distracted look, wiping her damp face with the back of her hand.

'I like the fringe,' he commented, a distinct twinkle in his blue eyes. 'I wondered if you'd keep it.'

'It just happened to fall over my face. It isn't very practical for the office.'

'Why ever not?' He pushed her hair into better shape, giving his full concentration to the task. 'It wants to be a little shorter. Have you a pair of scissors?'

'You're not going to cut it!' She took a step away from

48

him, catching up her handbag from the desk and clutching it to her. 'You might do it all wrong!'

He eased the bag out of her clasp, amused by her reaction. 'What else do you keep in your purse?' he asked her. 'A tissue wouldn't come amiss. You've blotched your eye-shadow when you were crying about nothing.'

'Oh, do I look awful?' She tried to take her bag back so that she could take a look at herself in the mirror inside, but he held on to it, opening it carefully and searching for the scissors. He found them with a triumphant look at her and snapped the bag shut again.

'You look cute!' he assured her. He turned her round to face him with an air of purpose from which there seemed to be no mistake. 'Look up, honey, or I may cut your eyelashes off by mistake!'

She did so, determined to tell him what she thought of men who looked uninvited into ladies' handbags, but, when it came to it, she never said a word. It wouldn't have made any difference if she had, she told herself. He would have gone his own way just the same.

'I'm not the only one to find you intimidating!' she burst out. 'Fatemeh does too.'

'Do I know Fatemeh?'

She nodded, only to be rewarded by a swift tug at her hair, forcing her face upwards again. 'She runs the typing pool. She came up to help me with this.' She waved her hand in the direction of the piles of papers still awaiting filing.

He pulled her hair down over her eyes and snipped away without answering. 'There!' he said at last, examining the results with a pleased smile. 'Since when did you find me intimidating?'

'From the first moment I met you!'

'Is that what it was? I thought you rather liked being swept off your feet.'

'Well, I didn't!' she denied.

The expression in his eyes openly mocked her. 'Is Madam pleased with her new style?' He put his head on one side and considered her appearance. 'It'll do, I think. It suits you, and it's short enough now for you not to have to peer through it like an overgrown Yorkshire

49

terrier.'

'Do you mind! What do you know about Yorkshires anyway?'

He looked at her solemnly. 'We have dogs in America too,' he said.

She flushed, feeling foolish. 'I know that! But I can't see you with a dog somehow. It wouldn't fit in with your way of life.'

'True, but I may change my mind any time now. There was a time when I thought all men who worked abroad should live alone, but now I'm not so sure. What do you think about that?'

Stephanie pulled the glass out of her bag and studied herself for a long moment before replying. She looked completely different! Less the perfect secretary and more— More what? More like a girl who wanted to please, she thought, and was not very sure how to go about it. She looked—there was no doubt about it!—very much more like herself!

'I don't think anyone should live alone,' she said.

'And Iran is hardly the back of beyond these days,' he added, watching her closely.

'But you may not be here very long,' she objected. 'They may send you somewhere else and bring my father back to finish here.'

He took the mirror from her. 'No, they won't do that. Was that what all the tears were about, Stephanie? Were you missing your father?'

'Not really.' She was too honest to pretend about a thing like that. The memory of the letters she had found gave her a nasty jolt, though, and she wondered yet again what to do about them. 'Cas, how important is all this equipment to the project? Can we manage without it?'

'Not a hope. They're laying the cables now between the Russian border and the eastern part of the country, and the stocks are running low. Still, it isn't the only trouble we're having. Some of the nomads don't care for the way the wires sing when the wind gets into them. They think they're voices from another world and want them taken away. Sooner or later we may have to sort something out about that.' He grinned. 'If I go on tour, shall I take you with me?'

Her breath caught in her middle and her eyes were wide with excitement. 'Would you? Could you? I'd love to go *anywhere*!'

'It would mean roughing it,' he warned her. 'You like to have everything in apple-pie order, don't forget, and camping isn't always like that.'

'I should think it's more necessary than ever in difficult conditions,' she retorted. 'If everything is put away properly fewer things get lost. It stands to reason!'

'So it does!' he teased her. 'You haven't said what you think of your new hair-style.'

'Haven't I?' She averted her face, blushing a little. 'I like it. I didn't know you were a hairdresser as well as everything else.'

His smile grew wider. 'I wanted to change your style right from the start!' He looked up as there was a knock at the door. 'Come in!' He was not smiling now. On the contrary, he looked downright grim.

The door opened a few inches to admit the most beautiful girl Stephanie had ever seen. She crossed the room with sinuous grace, her feet completely silent, with eyes only for Cas. Voluptuous was the adjective that first came to mind, with a fantastic, curvaceous figure that bordered dangerously on being overweight, but so far was just teetering on the brink of a description that Stephanie knew without being told would reduce the figure's owner to hysterical despair.

'Meet Amber,' he invited Stephanie laconically.

Stephanie shot him a bewildered glance. 'Amber?'

'My professional name,' the girl put in with a complacent smile. 'I'm a singer.'

'She dances too,' Cas added.

'The two go together,' Amber retorted. 'You may see me anywhere in the Middle East. I am very much in demand!'

'Yes, but what is your real name?' Stephanie asked.

Amber shrugged her magnificent shoulders. 'It's too long ago for me to remember. Amber is more me. My other name didn't suit me at all.' She managed to drag her eyes away from Cas's face and stared with surprise first at Stephanie and then at the little pile of hair on the

51

floor. 'What strange things one does in offices nowadays!'

'We had a burglar,' Stephanie muttered.

'So I see. What else was taken besides pieces of your hair?'

'Oh, that!' Stephanie raised a muted laugh. 'That was Cas—Mr. Ruddock, I mean. He was giving me a haircut.'

'And you allowed him to? The result might have been quite—odd, don't you think? He has never to my knowledge cut a girl's hair before!'

'There's a first time for everything,' Cas put in. 'Did you want something, Amber?'

'You, darling, what else? But now I'm here I'd like to hear all about this burglar of yours. Is this the only office he broke into?'

'So far as we know,' Cas answered her. 'It's a storm in a teacup. Stephanie makes too much of it. It hasn't done her temper any good to have to spend the afternoon clearing things up in here.' He put an easy arm around Amber's waist and led her towards the door. 'What do you do when I don't feed you? Does the management allow you to starve when you sing and dance so nicely for them?'

'Of course not, but I prefer to eat with you, darling. You always give me an appetite—and not only for food!'

'A likely tale!' said Cas. He turned back to Stephanie in the doorway. 'Don't forget the lift,' he reminded her yet again. 'And don't stay on here by yourself getting yourself into a gloomy mood. Nobody's blaming you.'

Stephanie turned her back on him. She didn't want to have to watch him go with Amber tucked under his arm when that was where she wanted to be herself and, more than anything, she didn't want to go home alone knowing that he was taking some other girl to dinner. And what a girl! Where could he have found such a dish as Amber undoubtedly was when he had hardly had a minute to himself since coming to Isfahan? But perhaps he had known her before? Perhaps he knew her very well? And even if he didn't, but had only just met her, it meant that he was unlikely to have much time to spend with his inherited secretary from now on. How could she help being gloomy with such a thought to go home with?

52

She put the letters of her father's she had found at the very bottom of the file and locked the drawer, determined not to think about them again until the next day. After a good night's sleep she might even know what to do about them. Perhaps the simplest solution would be to mail them to her father just as they were and leave him to worry about them. In fact she would have done that there and then if she hadn't been conscious of a feeling of disloyalty to Cas and, for some reason that she couldn't understand, she felt Cas needed her loyalty even more than her father did.

When she went downstairs she told Ali about the lift and told him to summon an engineer to get it put right.

'But, Miss Black, every lift in Isfahan—'

Stephanie smiled sweetly at him. '*You* tell that to Mr. Ruddock, Ali.'

'He will find out, Miss Black. I have never known a lift not have these little difficulties. They are all the same. We call the engineer for one fault and before he has gone again we have another one.'

'I know, Ali, I know. But Mr. Ruddock doesn't appreciate getting an electric shock every time he presses one of the buttons. The engineer will have to settle for another fault that Mr. Ruddock won't notice.'

Ali produced a sheepish smile. 'If you say so, Miss Black. You will be very pleased I know to have it put right. You are not liking electric shocks either!'

'No, I'm not!' she agreed. 'If you could get it seen to before tomorrow—'

Ali shook his head very slowly from side to side. 'Who will come to deal with such a small matter before tomorrow or the next day?' he demanded.

Stephanie basely fell back on the awed reception she knew her employer to have received by everyone who had seen him that day. 'Mr. Ruddock will expect us to do better than that when he complains about something. He won't be very pleased if he presses the button and gets another shock tomorrow.'

Ali's confidence was shaken. 'I will see what I can do, Miss Black,' he promised.

After that, there was no further reason why Stephanie

shouldn't go home. She still had many of her things to arrange in her new apartment and, if she had nothing better to do, she could try out her new Persian recipe and make herself a feast to eat all by herself. The programme wasn't as attractive as it should have been. She had never minded her own society before, but then she hadn't often had to suffer it. There had always been her father to talk to, or her mother, or one of her many friends who were always in and out of the house back home in England.

The truth was, she told herself severely, that it wasn't her own company that was like a sour taste in her mouth, but the company Cas was keeping that evening. To her jaundiced imagination, Amber seemed to be everything that she was not. Beautiful, glamorous, and highly desirable in every way! What man could resist her? What man would want to?

Stephanie always liked the moment when she stepped out of the office building into the street. She would check off the numbers on the trees as she walked beneath them on her way home. Indeed, she had first learned to read Persian numerals because of her interest in the trees. She had wondered why they should be numbered at all and, when she had discovered that it was to check that each treee had its fair ration of water, as well as checking that no one had taken an axe to one or two while nobody had been looking, she had started checking up on them herself, sometimes having to jump over the rushing water as it was allowed to run through the gulleys that ran between the pavements and the road.

Only tonight when she stepped out into the street, Gloria was waiting for her.

'I thought you wouldn't want to be on your own this evening,' the other girl greeted her. 'You've had quite a day, haven't you? I say, did you see the girl-friend who went up to find Mr. Ruddock? She's certainly dished any hopes you or I might have had of attracting his attention to ourselves. She looked so *available*, if you know what I mean?'

Stephanie did. 'I suppose Fatemeh has already gone?' she said.

'She never keeps her escort waiting long. Today I got

down early myself and saw her wrapping herself up in her veil. Funny really, her brother has quite modern ideas about women, but he doesn't see anything peculiar in his sister going around in a veil in this day and age. Nobody would get me into one, and I told him so!'

'Fatemeh said you knew one of her brothers,' Stephanie murmured, wondering how she was going to get through a whole evening of Gloria's undiluted society. 'Have you met the rest of her family?'

Gloria made a face at her. 'Me? It would be easier to break into the Bank of England than to be asked to visit some of these families. The women have a rotten time of it, never going anywhere, while the men have all the fun.' She glanced up and down the street. 'Have you anything to eat at your place? We could eat out if you haven't, but I'd rather not. It isn't any fun when there aren't any men around, is it?'

Stephanie seldom ate out. Being a good cook and an economical one, she preferred to prepare her own food, but even if she hadn't she would have resented the cost of eating in restaurants except for special occasions. Like last night, she thought dolefully, and was shaken to feel a barb of jealousy that it was not she who was eating with Cas Ruddock tonight.

'What's the matter?' Gloria asked curiously. 'You've gone quite white.'

'Have I? I was just thinking. Of course you must come home with me and I'll try out a new recipe on you. You can tell me what you think of it. I haven't completely settled in to my new apartment—it's more a room with mod. cons—but I think it's fairly tidy.'

'Okay,' said Gloria, 'let's do that. But can you hang on for a moment? I've left my book upstairs and I may want it to read myself to sleep later on.'

Stephanie wiped her face clear of all expression in case she should look as startled as she felt at the idea of Gloria reading anything, let alone taking a book to work with her! 'I'll wait here,' she said.

Gloria was gone a long time. Stephanie stood first on one foot and then on the other, longing to get home. It had been quite a day and she was tired. It had been more of a strain than she had allowed working for Cas for the first time, but she had learned a lot from him too. It had been a revelation to find a mind as clear and concise as his, after the muddled thinking of her father, and her own love of order had instantly responded to the challenge giving her a glow of satisfaction that she had been able to keep up with him all through the morning. If it had not been disloyal to her father, she would not have hesitated to admit that she infinitely preferred working for the American and not only because she was attracted to him as a man. Indeed, it had been in spite of it, for she, like him, was a firm believer in leaving one's personal life outside the office doors. If one could, she added with an uncomfortable spurt of self-criticism. It was becoming harder and harder to see Cas as anything else but the most attractive man she had ever known.

Gloria came back breathless and laughing. 'The lift is out of action. Someone was fool enough to complain of getting an electric shock when he—or I'll bet it was a she—pressed the button to go up or down. They'll learn! I never have any trouble! I always press it before I take off my gloves!'

'I don't wear gloves when it's hot,' Stephanie remarked, not wanting to get further involved, but Gloria was not easily diverted once she was following a line of thought.

'I'll bet it was Casimir's dreamboat who complained!'

'No, it wasn't!' Stephanie was horrified to hear the note of pain in her voice. 'It wasn't,' she said more calmly. 'It was Mr. Ruddock himself who ordered it to be seen to. I think he's used to everything around him working like clockwork.'

'His secretary too?' Gloria nodded wisely. 'I know the type. I'm glad *I* don't have to work for him. I don't know that I'd like to play with him either. He kind of likes to have his own way, doesn't he?'

'No more than the rest of us,' Stephanie smiled.

'Well, he doesn't mind putting you in an awkward position,' Gloria rushed on heedlessly. 'You must be torn in two when he reverses all your father's decisions. What will you do if you have to choose between them?'

Pray God, it never came to that! 'I won't ever have to,' Stephanie maintained. 'I'm only the secretary, not the
56

board of directors!'

'Even so, it must be hard to listen to him criticising your father. I wouldn't like that! I think I'd pack up and go back to England myself, sooner than get involved in anything like that!'

Stephanie stiffened. 'I can't imagine Mr. Ruddock criticising my father to my face!'

'It would depend what he found out about him.' Gloria's winning smile was designed to take any offence out of her words. 'I *liked* him, as I told you, but he must have done something to have been sent back to England at a moment's notice. He wasn't clever enough to cook the books, but he must have done *something*!'

One thing he could have done would have been to curb Gloria's tongue, but the idea of her easy-going father doing anything as positive as checking anyone who worked for him brought a maternal smile to her lips. Poor Father! He couldn't be severe with anyone to save his life!

'He was needed in England,' Stephanie answered, hoping against hope that Gloria would believe her. 'Didn't you know? They're fighting for some other contract in Africa somewhere and my father was needed to work out the costs for them.'

'In Africa?' Gloria was plainly astonished. 'It's the first I've heard of it. Is it a private deal?'

'I don't know,' Stephanie said, already regretting what she knew to be a downright lie. 'Does it matter?'

'If it was up for public tender there would be other companies involved. We might not get it.'

'We might not get it anyway,' Stephanie pointed out. In fact they certainly wouldn't, for no such contract existed except in her imagination.

'It's probably a Commonwealth country,' Gloria said knowledgeably. 'They prefer to have British equipment. It fits in better with what they already have. Isn't it odd that they should send an American to lord it over us here? That's the trouble with working for an international company, you never know what you're going to get! I used to work for a completely British company before I came here, but they sold out to another international combine. It's the modern trend!'

Stephanie tried to pretend that she had never heard of such a trend before, but was visibly relieved when they reached the block where both her new and her old apartments were situated.

'The best thing about my new room is that I have a splendid view of the dome of the Madrasseh of the Mother of the Shah. I think it one of the most beautiful I've seen.'

Gloria was unimpressed. 'They all look alike to me!' she declared. 'What's so special about this one?'

Stephanie unlocked her door and walked over to the window, allowing her eyes to rest on the delicate arabesques against the pale blue background with which the dome was decorated.

'I think it's the shape,' she said. 'It's such a pleasing shape, and the colours are superb! They're what I like best about Persian architecture. They float over the buildings, looking so right. One can see them from miles away, and yet they're just as remarkable when one is standing quite close to them. They never look out of place, but always seem to enhance the rest.'

'They're just buildings to me,' said Gloria. 'It isn't a very big room, is it?'

'Big enough,' Stephanie defended it. She wondered how big Gloria's was and doubted that it was any bigger. 'If you sit down, I'll pour you a drink. What will you have? I haven't got the ice-tray under control yet, but I have got some vodka my father left behind.'

'It'll have to do,' Gloria said without much enthusiasm. 'I don't much like these foreign drinks, do you?'

'What do you prefer?'

'I'd as soon have a glass of sherry as anything else,' Gloria answered, apparently blissfully unaware that sherry too was produced in a foreign country. 'Spirits go to my head. I always think they're better left to the men really.'

Stephanie handed her a vodka and lemon whether she wanted it or not and, feeling decidedly ruffled, took refuge in the tiny kitchen and began to prepare their meal. It was being slowly borne in on her that she didn't like Gloria Lake, never had liked her, and that it was extremely unlikely that she ever would like her. They hadn't a thing in common and she couldn't help wondering what had persuaded Gloria to take a job so far away from England, her family, and the local High Street which she suspected was the only place where the other girl was really at home.

When she went back to her guest, Gloria was sitting on the edge of the sofa, her drink in her hand. Stephanie had no reason for thinking so, but she was sure that Gloria had not been sitting there all the time she had been in the kitchen. A glance at her drink made her even more certain, for the liquid was rocking back and forth and yet had obviously not yet been tasted. Stephanie took an oblique look round the room and was annoyed to see that she had left out a letter she was writing to her mother. She rather hoped Gloria had not been reading it, because it had contained a plea that her mother should welcome home her father with open arms. She had begun to write it after she had seen her father off at the airport and had thought he had looked so sad and old, but later in the evening, after Cas had seen her home, she had decided against sending it as it was and had almost decided to rewrite it without making any reference to her father at all.

She knew in her heart of hearts that she would have sent the letter if Cas hadn't told her to leave well alone as far as her parents were concerned. It was yet one more thing to bother her that where Cas was concerned she seemed well content to measure her judgement against his and to accept his dictums with a meekness that she had never noticeably displayed with any other man, her father included. It was hard to believe that she had only met the American for the first time the day before. It felt as though he had always been there and she had to admit that she liked the feeling.

Sitting down in the chair opposite Gloria, Stephanie knew that the evening was not going to be a success. Gloria probably had no taste for rice, even rice as good as the Iranian variety was, and even less was she likely to enjoy the pomegranate sauce she had prepared to go with the pieces of chicken she had had waiting in the refrigerator. Still, as there was nothing else for them to eat there was nothing she could do about it, but she couldn't help contrasting today's meal with the one she

59

had eaten the night before.

She was amused to find she had summed up Gloria Lake with an accuracy that would have appealed to her mother's ironic sense of humour. The other girl was obviously appalled to be presented with a plateful of fluffy white rice and the chicken, simmering in the pomegranate sauce, brought a look of such acute distaste to her face that Stephanie felt quite sorry for her. However, by burying most of her chicken under the rice, Gloria did what she could to put a good face on things. She even managed a sheepish smile as Stephanie cleared away the plates, excusing her own with an apologetic, 'Leave some for Mr. Manners!'

Stephanie suppressed a delighted giggle and almost ran into the kitchen. She could only hope that Gloria would like the second course of fresh fruit salad better than she had the first. But Gloria hastily refused anything further, claiming that she had always had a very small appetite and that Stephanie was not to mind if she didn't eat as heartily as Stephanie obviously did.

Fortunately, Stephanie was saved from the impossible task of having to answer that by an imperative knock on the door. Excusing herself with a lighthearted smile which she hoped concealed the unholy joy she felt at the interruption, Stephanie went to the door and opened it wide. She was astonished to see Cas's enormous frame on the other side, smiling at her quite as widely as she was at him.

'Where's Amber?' she said before she had thought.

'I mislaid her on the dance floor about half an hour ago.'

'How—how careless!'

'Wasn't it?' His smile grew into a complacent grin. 'Aren't you going to invite me in?'

She stood back to allow him to enter. 'Gloria Lake is here,' she warned him in an undertone.

'Is she now?' His eyebrows shot upwards in comic disbelief. 'I hadn't realised you were friends?'

'She came to supper,' Stephanie said more loudly. 'Did you want something, Mr. Ruddock?'

The appreciative look he gave her made her blush scarlet, but he said nothing, and she thought she would love him for ever when he met the naked curiosity in Gloria's eyes with a pleasant nod and turned straight back to Stephanie.

'What I need is a beer, honey,' he said, dropping into the nearest chair. 'It's been a long, hard evening.' He surveyed his secretary with a very masculine look and stood up again. 'On second thoughts, you look a bit frayed yourself. I'll go and forage in the ice-box for my own beer. Okay with you?'

'Yes, of course,' she said quickly.

'I'd better go,' Gloria hissed across the room as he disappeared into the kitchen. 'I had no idea things were like that between you. Why didn't you tell me?'

'There's nothing to tell!' Stephanie said weakly.

'No?' said Gloria. 'I'll go anyway.' She gathered up her things with a disapproving sniff and walked quickly towards the door. 'I don't like this sort of hole and corner business, but it won't do any harm to wish you good luck. Having seen the opposition, I think you're going to need it!'

CHAPTER V

Cas emerged from the kitchen triumphant, a can of beer in his hand.

'Just testing your domestic organisation,' he teased her. 'You've underrated my capacity, though. I can get through your whole supply in a single evening.'

'I didn't get it in for you!'

His confidence was undaunted. 'No? Are you a secret beer drinker, my love?'

'I had it for my father,' she said repressively. How like him, she thought, to walk in on her when she was least expecting him and to take command of her arrangements as though he had every right to do so and without so much as a by your leave! Didn't he know that he had set the office tongues gossiping about the two of them, for the chances were thin that Gloria would keep such a spicy item to herself?

'I never doubted it,' he drawled. 'Want some?'

She shook her head. 'I don't like it.' She sounded as stuffy as she felt, but she didn't care. If he didn't like the coolness of her welcome, he could always go back to Amber!

'I came for a reason,' he said. He folded his length into the corner of the sofa and patted the vacant seat beside him. 'I started to think about you, honey, and I don't think you're the sort to cry about nothing. What was it all about?'

'Nothing.' Now she sounded sulky as well as everything else, she thought in despair.

'There's nothing you want to tell me about?'

He patted the seat beside him again and she sat down quickly, almost collapsing on to the sofa, because her knees felt suddenly weak and quite unable to support her. The dreadful thing was that if she didn't make an effort now he would *know*—Only there was nothing to know, because she wasn't sure herself, at least, she wasn't completely sure. How could she be? Nothing like this had ever happened to her before!

She cast him a confused glance from beneath her

lashes and as promptly wished she hadn't, for the look in his bright blue eyes had a chaotic effect on her mental processes, sending her into a delicious panic. She should have sat further away from him, *anything* rather than betray to him the effect he was having on her.

'What did you really do with Casimir's dreamboat?' she asked him, no longer sounding either stuffy or sulky.

'With *what*?'

She lowered her eyes, looking demure. 'That was Gloria's name for her. Did you really lose her on the dance floor?'

'She isn't the kind to be short of partners,' he answered dryly. 'I'll take you to see her act one of these days, if you like? She's quite something!'

Stephanie could imagine! 'I suppose you've known her a long time?' she said carefully.

He put a finger under her chin and turned her face towards him. 'A couple of years. I met her first in Beirut, and I've seen her from time to time ever since. Anything else you want to know?'

Yes! She passionately wanted to know what Amber meant to him. She wasn't the sort of person that any man could contemplate with only platonic friendship in mind. She was far too beautiful for that! Too beautiful and too exotic by far!

'I suppose not,' she said.

He picked up his can of beer and poured some of the frothy fluid straight down his throat, without troubling to pour it into a glass. 'Amber would be flattered,' he said.

She didn't know what he meant by that. She watched, fascinated, the smooth, tanned column of his throat as the beer disappeared without his seeming to swallow even once.

'How do you do that?' she demanded.

'It's an old college trick.' He smiled at her, his eyes bright. 'You shouldn't tempt me to show off. If you look at me like that, I might be tempted to try out another trick or two I have up my sleeve.'

She looked away hastily, her breath catching in her throat. 'Like what?'

He grinned. 'I think it's a bit soon to give you a demonstration. Besides, if you don't like beer, I'll drink something else before I show you what I mean. I don't want to give you a distaste of me!'

She was unaccountably disappointed. The colour came and went in her cheeks as she made a determined effort to pretend that she hadn't understood him.

'You shouldn't have come here!' she burst out with a petulance of which she had not known herself capable. 'Gloria will spread it all over the office that you're interested in me!'

'So I am.' He frowned. 'Are you ashamed of being seen with me?'

'Of course not!'

'Then I don't see your problem.' His very gentleness disturbed her more than his anger would have done. 'Do you want me to go?'

'No,' she admitted.

'Good.' He relaxed completely, with his long legs stuck out in front of him, and shut his eyes. 'Gloria would gossip about us whatever we do, partly because she's the type, and partly because she's jealous of you. If I were you, I shouldn't get too friendly with her. She'll make your life a misery if you let her. I've seen her kind before.'

She opened her eyes wide, deliberately mocking him. 'In America?'

'You meet the same types all over the world, my dear, *especially* in America, and especially on the distaff side.'

'I suppose you've met my type before too,' she said huffily.

He opened his eyes and smiled at her, watching the colour edge up her neck and face. 'Not quite like you,' he drawled. 'And believe me, I'd have noticed if I had!'

'No English roses?' she pressed him.

He studied her thoughtfully. 'Are there honey-coloured roses? I think you're a less obvious flower altogether. Perhaps not a flower at all, but a sheaf of corn, like one of those delightful corn-dollies that country people make. Highly decorative!'

She made no effort to hide her pleasure at the compliment. 'Perhaps I'm more complicated than you think,' she murmured.

'Corn-dollies come in some very intricate designs,' he answered.

64

She hesitated, feeling unaccountably guilty. 'Cas, do you ever wonder if you're doing the right thing? I mean, do you always put your loyalty to your work first?'

'I put it before my own comfort.'

That gave her a jolt. Was it more comfortable to *think* she was being loyal to her father, when perhaps she ought to trust him more? Was she only afraid of the hornet's nest she might stir up by telling Cas about the letters? But supposing, just supposing her father had written the letters and she were the one to bring it to the company's attention. Would she ever be able to forgive herself?

'Well?' he prompted her.

She shook her head. 'I have to work it out for myself,' she said.

'But you'd tell me if you told anyone?'

'Yes—yes, I would!'

'Okay,' he said, 'I'll be content with that. I can wait.'

'But how do you know you can trust me?' she fretted. 'Half of me doesn't think I'm right at all! Only—'

'I'd trust you against pretty long odds. You'll tell me when you're good and ready.'

She didn't know how he could be so certain. 'I may never tell you. I hope I won't have to!'

'If it concerns your father, so do I! You look tired, my dear. How about leaving everything for now and getting an early night?'

'I haven't done the washing up!'

He stood up immediately. 'I'll give you a hand,' he volunteered. He pulled her to her feet, combing her fringe into position with his fingers. 'I wonder if I ought to make you tell me now, away from the office,' he mused. 'It may be that Cas can be a great deal more sympathetic to your cause than Mr. Ruddock will be able to be. I'm not my own master when I'm on duty, my dear.'

'I shouldn't expect any favours from you—*ever*!' she insisted.

The smile he gave her was decidedly wry. 'You might not expect it, but I should find it very hard not to do my best to protect you, no matter what the circumstances.' He took her hands in his, looking down at her neatly shaped nails and the network of little lines that crisscrossed her palms. 'You have more power than you know,' he said finally. 'Use it wisely, little one.'

Stephanie wasn't accustomed to having anyone to help her with the washing-up. Cas gave the impression of filling the whole kitchen as he stood beside her at the sink, accepting the soapy dishes from her hand and drying them carefully before placing them on the table for her to put away.

'You ought to rinse them if you want to stay healthy,' he told her. 'The best way is to have a double sink, like we have back home, then all you have to do is to slip the dishes out of the detergent and into the plain water to rinse them.'

'You sound as though you wash-up all the time,' she said.

'Why not? I eat all the time too!' He sniffed appreciatively at the remains of the chicken dish, sticking a finger into it and tasting it thoughtfully with his head on one side. 'Not bad at all!' he commented. 'It's a darned sight better than the mess Amber and I were served tonight.'

'At your hotel?'

'No, not there! I moved out of there this morning and into your erstwhile apartment. No, Amber feels she might be recognised if she goes anywhere anyone has ever heard of. Tonight's retreat was an all-time low!' His eyes met hers with a flash of amusement. 'You didn't miss a thing!'

She turned on both taps so that she wouldn't have to answer and was hardly surprised at all when he reached over and turned them off again. 'I'm washing! You're supposed to be drying!' she rebuked him.

'Very unhygienic! One ought really to leave them to drain!'

'I haven't the space! Besides, I didn't ask you to help! I'd just as soon you went and sat down and left me to it. It would feel a lot less crowded, if you want to know. I might even have room to breathe!'

He turned her round forcibly to face him, taking first the plate she was holding and dropping it into the bowl of water and then the cloth which he threw into the corner of the sink.

66

'Stephanie, don't try me too far!' he warned her. 'What do you suppose you do to my breathing?' He looked down at her agitated face and lifted her clear off her feet until she could look him straight in the eyes. Only she didn't feel able to look at him at all! She wriggled her toes and her shoes fell off with a little plop. He gave no sign of even noticing. His blue eyes blazed with sudden emotion and he kissed her very gently full on the lips. 'And don't pretend you don't like it!' he commanded her with a masterful air. 'You like it every bit as much as I do!'

He put her back on her feet, pushed her fringe back into position one last time with a proprietorial hand, and walked out of the kitchen. He didn't even hurry. Stephanie heard the front door shut behind him, but she made no attempt to move. If she hadn't known it before, she knew it now. She was in acute danger of falling deeply and irrevocably in love with Casimir Ruddock! And she was very much afraid that he knew it too.

It was too early in the morning for there to be many people in the courtyard of the College of the Mother of the Shah. Stephanie had woken early and had spent nearly an hour watching the sun come up through the rosy glow of dawn behind the dome of the College. Her thoughts were too uncomfortable for her to want to dwell on them. Indeed, she seemed to have spent most of the night worrying about the letters she had found, wishing she had confided in Cas when he had first given her the opportunity, and then falling into a fit of despair when she considered what the future held for her. It had made for a very long night and she had been quite glad to see the darkness finally give way to the pale light of day.

She had made herself some coffee and had thought about going back to bed, but the relative smallness of her new apartment, which hadn't mattered at all until that moment, seemed suddenly oppressive and, without conscious volition, she had started off down the street and had found herself outside the magnificent silver doors of the Madrasseh itself. For a moment she thought it might be locked, but the door opened to her touch and she slipped into the shadowed interior with a sense of wonder. She had half expected that she would be disappointed in the building that supported the dome she had come to love. Instead she was overwhelmed by the charm of its setting, and she was no longer surprised that it had been described to her as the last of the truly great buildings of the Safavid period in Iran.

The College had been built between the years of 1706–14, under the patronage of the mother of Shah Sultan Husain, as a seminary for theological students. Nowadays, although the place is still open for prayer, there are no students left. The building has been magnificently restored, however, from the ruin it had become, and Stephanie was well content to wander through the stalactite-vaulted *iwan* and into the vaulted octagonal vestibule where stands a huge stone basin used for ritual ablutions. It was the main court that she liked best of all for, instead of the usual paving stones, she found herself in a delightful garden, set about with pools that reflected in their depths both the building and the white-stemmed *chinars* which shaded the open space from the rigours of the noonday sun in summer.

Stephanie was still standing, looking around her, when a small figure came up to her out of the shadows, allowing her *chador* to fall away from her face to reveal a welcoming smile.

'I have never seen you here before!' Fatemeh greeted her. 'It is lovely at this time of day, isn't it?'

'I should think it's lovely at any time of the day!' Stephanie exclaimed.

'Yes, but it is nicer before the tourists come and all one can hear is the clicking of cameras and bright, brittle voices!'

Stephanie gave the Persian girl a startled look. 'Is that how we sound to you?' she asked.

Fatemeh nodded regretfully. 'I expect we often sound strident to you, though, don't we?'

'Not to me personally,' Stephanie denied.

'But then not all Europeans make noises like birds,' Fatemeh laughed at her. 'I have never heard you giggle and gossip as Gloria does, and who can imagine Mr. Ruddock talking other than like this?' She gave a very creditable imitation of Cas's deep voice slightly slurring his consonants, especially the 't's and 'd's, so that they were indistinguishable to an English ear.

Stephanie giggled then. 'Can you imitate everyone as well as that?' she asked.

Fatemeh looked pleased. 'It's my—how do you say it? —my party trick!' She lifted her voice almost an octave, setting her mouth in a tight, round shape. 'Have you ever seen anything *like* our Mr. Ruddock? He doesn't set *my* heart beating any faster, of course, but do you *know*, Miss Black actually allowed him to trim her hair! I think there must be *something* there, don't you?'

Stephanie could feel herself blushing. 'I'd like to see *her* stop Mr. Ruddock doing anything he had set his mind on—'

'But it looks pretty, Stephanie! Why should you pay any attention to anything Gloria says? We all know what she is like.'

Stephanie couldn't help remembering Gloria as she had last seen her, and her mouth had been exactly as Fatemeh had betrayed it, and her eyes full of jealous dislike for herself. She shivered, feeling suddenly cold. No one had ever disliked her before that she could remember, not with the implacable malice that she had seen on Gloria's face last night, and she wondered what she could have done to the other girl to have inspired such hatred.

'I wish I liked her better,' she sighed.

But Fatemeh was unimpressed. 'She doesn't wish you to like her. Surely you know that? When she came out here she expected to work for the top man, but your father brought you with him, and now, when she might have replaced you with Mr. Ruddock, he seems more than content with you—in and out of the office!'

'He's no more than friendly! Americans have a gift for getting on quickly with other people. They don't need time to get to know one, like we in England do!'

'And we in Iran! We are very good to foreigners—we never shot them, not even when we were still fighting, one village against the next, all the time. But we suspect all strangers to the very last, until they have proved themselves to us!'

'Then you must suspect me?' Stephanie challenged her, but Fatemeh only laughed at the thought.

'You have never been a stranger, Stephanie. I have always felt at home with you!'

Stephanie's eyes misted, feeling as though she had had a medal pinned on her. 'I thought I had the reputation for being stand-offish and aloof?'

'Not amongst us Iranians. How could you think that?'

Stephanie knew very well why she had thought it. 'I don't know, I just did,' she said. She was tempted to tell Fatemeh about her evening the night before, if only to spike Gloria's guns before she got busy regaling the office with her version of what had happened. But how was she to explain Cas's visit even to Fatemeh? She couldn't explain it to herself! All she knew was that she had only to think of him standing beside her at the sink in her tiny kitchen for her heart to go into an acrobatic, swooping action that made her feel quite dizzy and peculiar, and quite unlike her usual orderly, slightly staid and even more serious self.

'Do you come here often?' she said instead.

Fatemeh chuckled. 'All the time. I come for the morning prayer when I want to be alone. It will not be long now before I am to marry, and it is good to prepare oneself well for our new life.' She turned impulsively to Stephanie. 'Will you come to my wedding? I should like you to be there! It will be such a happy day for me!'

'Thank you, I'd love to. I didn't know you were getting married.

Fatemeh nodded. 'My parents arranged it many years ago. I have seen him sometimes when he has come home with my brothers. He is very handsome! He is a civil engineer and very clever! When he finished at university he had to spend some years working for a village community as his national service and to repay to the country the cost of his education, but now he can work anywhere and there is nothing to delay our marriage.'

'But are you in love with him?' Stephanie asked.

'I shall be when I know him better. He is right for me, and I know that I like him. Our families have always been friendly together. That is a good thing when two people are to marry.'

'I'd want to be in love before I married anyone,' Stephanie mused. 'And I'd want him to be in love with me!'

Fatemeh looked wise. 'It is different for you,' she said. 'You meet and talk to many men and so it is easy to decide for yourself whom you shall marry, but it is all the same in the end, I think. However often you meet a man, you cannot know what it will be like to be married to him until you are his wife. What more do you know about Mr. Ruddock than I know about my fiancé?'

Stephanie's heart missed a beat. What did she know about Cas Ruddock? Only that he was the most wonderful person in the world!

'Mr. Ruddock—'

Fatemeh giggled, well satisfied with her friend's reaction. 'I have seen the way he looks at you! For once the imaginative Miss Gloria Lake is right! There is *something* between you, no? You like him very much?'

'Very much,' Stephanie admitted.

Fatemeh giggled again. 'That is how I like the man I am to marry too! But I am more fortunate, having my family to arrange it all for me, while you must wait for Mr. Ruddock to decide it all for you.' She put her head on one side, her eyes as bright as a bird's. 'Or has he already made up his mind to have you?'

Stephanie presented a scarlet face. 'Of course not! He doesn't think about me like that at all! He's my employer —nothing more than that!'

Fatemeh drew the loose flap of her *chador* across her face, holding it in place with her teeth while she adjusted the folds of her skirt. 'So,' she teased, 'you think of him just like you think of your father—'

'Fatemeh!'

The Persian girl shook her head at her, her eyes flashing with laughter. 'You mustn't mind my knowing, Stephanie. Your secret is safe with me! And Mr. Ruddock he already knows, doesn't he?'

'I hope not!' Stephanie gasped.

'But why? He is a kind man and he knows you are alone here and he won't take advantage of you.' She frowned, looking thoughtful. 'If you are afraid of that, I will ask my father to speak to him for you—'

71

'No, please don't!' Stephanie was appalled by the very idea.

'Well,' Fatemeh shrugged, 'you have only to ask!'

'Yes, thank you,' Stephanie said weakly, 'but Cas would think I'd gone mad! I hardly know him, after all!'

'It's not necessary to know well to like what one has seen,' Fatemeh retorted. 'You liked Isfahan the first day you were here!' She shrugged again. 'Have you been up on the roof? It's beautiful up there! Would you like to go?'

It was indeed beautiful. Seen through a silver filigree of *chinar*, the tile-work glowed almost as if it were alive, and was perfectly reflected in the absolutely still pools below.

'One never comes to the end of Isfahan!' Stephanie said dreamily. 'You are lucky to live here all the time!'

'There is nowhere else I want to live,' Fatemeh agreed. 'When I am married, I shall have to go away from time to time, but I shall always come back here. I want my children to be Isfahanis too. They do not speak such beautiful Farsi in other cities. It is important to know beauty when one is young and then it grows inside one all one's life!'

Perhaps that was true, Stephanie reflected. When the time came, she would hate to leave, that she did know. Isfahan would always hold a corner of her heart, and it couldn't be entirely, because it was there that she had met Casimir Ruddock. She wouldn't allow herself to think that! But her cheeks burned nevertheless and she made a play of admiring a new view of the tiled dome that had become so familiar to her in case the other girl should notice her confusion.

'We must go to work,' Fatemeh broke in on her thoughts. 'If you will walk with me, I'll send my maid home. She's waiting for me downstairs.'

Stephanie was intrigued. 'Do you never go anywhere alone?' she asked.

'I am fond of my maid. She has looked after me since I was a little child. I should be lonely without her. It's much nicer to do things in company. I like to have a lot of people around me.'

Certainly there was nothing servile about the maid's

attitude to her young mistress. She issued a spate of commands that Fatemeh listened to with her usual calm expression, nodding her head at intervals in agreement.

'She hasn't entirely accustomed herself to my working,' she explained as the two girls walked together down the street. 'She was harder to persuade than my parents were that it would be good for me to see the new world we are creating here. She still would prefer me to be at home like my sisters and entertain my friends for tea!'

'What about after you marry?'

'I shall have my husband's home to look after,' Fatemeh said with dignity.

Stephanie knew a moment's envy of the Persian girl. She could think of nothing she would like better than to look after the home of the man she loved. She would do it well too! She would make a much better housewife than secretary, she thought ruefully.

The lift was still out of order. Ali came forward with a long and detailed explanation of what the electrician had done to cure the trouble but all to no avail. 'He is getting a new panel to put in instead of this bad one,' he added with an engaging grin. 'But with all the wires sticking out, it is now not safe to use at all!'

Stephanie returned his grin with a malicious smile of her own. 'And how long is it going to be before we can use it?' she asked.

Ali was undismayed by the implication that the electrician would make it as long as possible. '*Insha'allah,* all will be well tomorrow!'

'Or the day after that?' Stephanie retorted.

Ali allowed himself a pained shrug of his shoulders. '*Insha'allah,*' he repeated.

'Allah has nothing to do with it,' another voice said crisply behind them, and Cas emerged from the stricken lift with a quick smile for Stephanie. 'Fetch me a screwdriver and I'll do it myself!'

Stephanie started for the stairs, trying not to laugh, but he called her back, beckoning her into the lift beside him.

'I don't understand anything about electricity,' she told him hastily.

'You don't have to! All you have to do is hold what I

tell you to hold and pass me the screwdriver when I need it!'

'All right, just so long as you don't blow us all up!'

'Oh, ye of little faith!' he taunted her, making the most of his extra inches to look down his nose at her. 'Just for that, you can wait till the bitter end and we'll go up in the lift together!'

It was interesting to see how quickly he worked, his fingers confidently manipulating the tangle of wires that lay behind the panel, sorting them into their right groups with a speed and efficiency that delighted her. In no time at all he had the problem sorted out and was replacing the panel on the front, screwing it firmly back into the wall of the lift.

'Right,' he said to Ali, 'you can turn the current back on now.'

The Iranian hurried to do so and Cas pushed the button for their floor and the lift glided smoothly upwards without any further trouble. Cas leaned against the side and surveyed Stephanie with a slight smile. 'What are you giggling about, young lady? Didn't you think I could do it?'

'I never doubted it for a moment!'

He grinned at her. 'If you're going to tell other people what to do, it pays to be able to do it yourself.' He looked more closely at her. 'Sleep well?' he asked her.

'I woke early. I'm all right,' she added. 'You don't have to worry about me.'

'It's getting to be a habit,' he responded. 'You won't break me of it easily.'

But then she wouldn't want to! She felt immeasurably cheered as she walked away from him into her own office, searching in her bag for the key to the locked door. Without bothering to put away the last of the files, she cleared a place at her desk preparatory to typing the letters Cas had dictated to her the day before. But she found the clutter disturbing and, a little irritated by her own need to have everything neat and tidy around her, she stood up again and began to sort what remained of the papers, clearing them out of sight as fast as she could.

So intent was she on what she was doing that she

74

jumped when the intercom buzzed on her desk and Cas's voice came through, sounding stern and unfriendly.

'Come in here a moment, will you, Miss Black?'

She went at once, every instinct telling her that something was badly wrong. As she went into his room, she knew at once what it was. In his hand he held the letters which she had found the day before and had hidden in the bottom drawer of the file in her office, the letters which had included the one from her father cancelling the equipment they had been waiting for so long.

Cas was sitting at his desk, not looking at her. Then he turned the full force of his bright blue eyes on to her.

'Did you leave these on my desk?' he asked her. And then again, as the silence grew between them, 'Well, did you, Miss Black?'

CHAPTER VI

Her face was grey with shock. How could they possibly have got on his desk? She shook her head miserably.

'I hid them,' she confessed. 'I didn't want you to see them!'

'Well, it appears that somebody else did,' he said. 'You little fool, Stephanie! Why didn't you tell me about them the moment you found them?'

'I don't believe my father wrote them!'

'Don't you?' he said grimly. 'Then who did?'

It was the most important thing in the world that he should believe her. 'I didn't type them—'

'Are you quite sure of that?'

'Yes,' she said. 'I never saw them in my life before yesterday. Though they were typed on my machine—at least I think they were, and they have my initials on them. But I didn't type them, and I'm almost sure my father never dictated them either!'

'I see.' He was silent for a long moment. 'You realise I shall have to follow this up? I shall have to find out if they were ever sent out as coming from your father, and I'll have to send a full report back to London.'

'Yes,' she murmured.

'It puts your father in the front line of suspects as far as the culprit who overturned your office is concerned too.'

'Yes,' she said again.

'Why the devil didn't you tell me all about it last night as I asked you to?'

Stephanie licked her lips nervously. 'I don't know,' she managed. 'I didn't know what to do! But I realise I can't go on working for you—under the circumstances. I'll give you my letter of resignation later in the day.'

'Getting in first?' he jibed. 'Okay, Miss Black, it looks as though I shall have to do without you in the office. Now sit down, before you go and faint on me, and let's talk about you and me. Feeling better?'

If anything she felt worse. She hoped desperately she

was not going to faint. She sat up very straight and tried to think of something else besides the pounding in her head and the black spots before her eyes.

'Is there anything to talk about?' she asked.

He came round the desk and placing a hand firmly on the nape of her neck, ruthlessly pressed her head well down between her knees. 'Stephanie, my love, don't you know that modern young ladies take anything in their stride without swooning away? Smelling salts went out with Queen Victoria, and I haven't any feathers to burn under your nose either. Come on, nothing is so bad that we can't face it together!'

'But this has nothing to do with you!' she protested. 'Cas, you're breaking my neck!'

'You're lucky I didn't do so the moment you walked in here! I had hoped you trusted me—'

'I don't *know* you!' she pleaded. His hold on her neck was as relentless as ever and, far from feeling faint any more, she was getting crosser by the minute as she suspected that he was enjoying her discomfiture.

'That,' he said calmly, 'can be remedied.' He pressed her head still lower and then finally allowed her to assume a more upright position, smiling at the scarlet indignation on her face. 'How you hate to have your dignity upset!' he teased her. 'But at least you don't look as though you're going to faint on me any more!'

She eyed him resentfully, automatically rearranging her skirts and patting her hair back into position. 'There are times when you are very unlikeable!' she shot at him. His quiet acceptance of this unpalatable truth drove her into further, more reckless speech. 'I hate you!' she said with passion.

'Like hell you do!' he retorted.

She watched, fascinated, as he bent his head towards her, and was quite unbearably disappointed when he changed his mind and took up his position behind the desk again.

'This isn't the time or the place for our own affairs,' he said as he sat down. 'We'll sort them out somewhere else. Meanwhile, Miss Black, I am not going to accept your resignation, but I am going to suspend you from working in these premises pending my enquiry into these letters.

Now, think hard, Stephanie! Is there anything else I ought to know before I let you go?'

'*Yes*! *I* want to know how the letters got on your desk. I didn't put them there, so who did?'

'That's what I mean to find out.'

'How?'

He raised a thoughtful eyebrow. 'I'd like to think you trusted me to do my best for you. Is that asking too much?'

His blue eyes held hers and she had the strange sensation that he could look right inside her and could read her inmost feelings, feelings that she didn't understand herself they were still so new to her.

'Wh-what?' she said vaguely.

'I was asking if you could bring yourself to trust me to look after you?'

'Yes, of course.' She wrenched her eyes away from his with an effort. What on earth was she talking about? There was nothing 'of course' about it! He was a stranger, *an American*! And it didn't matter at all! She was fathoms deep in love with him and she'd trust him with the last breath in her body. 'What do you want me to do?'

'Give me your keys and go home until I come to you.'

She gave him an uncertain smile. 'What about your letters?'

'Fatemeh can do them. She'll have to take your place temporarily.' He stood up and she thought anew how large he was and that he only had to look at her for her heart to turn over inside her. It was only a physical attraction, an acute awareness of him as a man, that she had never experienced before, and she could only hope that she was not about to make a crashing fool of herself by having the sort of crush on him that she ought to have learned how to manage in her adolescent days.

'Why not Gloria?' she said in a commendably even voice.

'I think Fatemeh will suit me better.'

Stephanie stood up too. 'Fatemeh is getting married soon. She's invited me to her wedding. What will you do then?'

He put out a hand and cradled her cheek. 'I'll manage. Now give me the keys and we'll go along to your office

78

together and pick up your personal things. Do you think you can amuse yourself until lunchtime without going into a decline because I won't let you go on working?'

'I think so,' she said. 'I'm quite modern in some ways.'

He grinned. 'You could have fooled me!'

'Why? What's so old-fashioned about me?' she demanded. 'I can't see that there's anything to laugh about!'

'Can't you? That's because you can't see your face!' His laughter was very gentle, though, and she thought she would be hard to please indeed if she were to resent it. 'Go home, honey,' he went on, 'and cook us something delectable for our lunch, after which I'll take you out for the afternoon. Okay?'

She gave him a smile that was more than a little shy. 'I thought you'd be angry with me for not telling you about the letters. I'm sorry, Cas.'

'A little disappointed. But I'll win your trust yet, my love. I'm old-fashioned too, you see. I don't like to see too much independence in a woman, not when I'm there to do her worrying for her. I have my pride too!'

'But I'm a stranger to you,' she objected. 'Why should I depend on you when I'm the one who's in trouble?'

He ran his hand through her hair, mussing it up to his satisfaction. 'Can't you guess?'

She chewed at the inside of her lip, shaking her head, suddenly rather nervous of him. 'Please don't, Cas.'

'Meaning you can guess, but you're not going to be drawn?'

'Meaning that I like to keep my hair neat!' she retorted. 'I don't like it all over the place!'

His chuckle made her blush. 'I think it looks cute. It makes you look like a windswept child! And you ought to be grateful. It got you off the hook and you haven't had to admit a thing—not this time!' He threatened to tousle her hair once again, but she stepped back too quickly to allow it. 'I take a personal interest in how you keep your hair,' he teased her.

She was immediately indignant. 'That doesn't give you the right—' she began, the more heatedly as she made the discovery that she hadn't really minded half as much as she thought she should have done.

'It's a right I choose to take!' he countered, smiling.

She had no answer ready for him. She gave him a quick, frightened look; her mouth gone dry, wondering what other rights he might choose to take and, even more, whether her already weakened defences were going to stand the strain. If he were less attractive to her, or if she could meet him on equal terms—but, in her heart of hearts, she knew that none of these things would have made any difference at all. She had been lost from the first moment that the urge to please him had been stronger than her need for caution and an orderly existence. She, who had always taken the long view, was now incapable of seeing anything but him and, heaven knows, he was large enough to block out the rest of the world if he'd a mind to!

He smoothed her hair down again, still smiling. 'You'd better go before I think up something else to delay you. Shall I come down in the lift with you?'

She shook her head, a little shocked that he should suggest it. 'Of course not!' She felt faintly relieved that she should sound so decided and in command of herself. 'But, Cas, I'm sure my father *didn't* write those letters!'

'Would you have shown them to me if you had thought he had?'

Her eyes wavered in the face of the brilliant blue of his. 'I hope I would have done,' she said at last. 'I *think* I would have done so, but I'll never be absolutely sure. I can't forget he's my father!'

'I'm not likely to forget it either,' he assured her.

'No, but you'll do the right thing,' she sighed. 'I wish I could be certain that I would have done so too.'

He touched her mouth with the tips of his fingers to silence her. 'You'll do, honey! Though I could have wrung your neck with the greatest of pleasure when I saw those letters on my desk this morning! You beguile me far too easily. Will you always do so, I wonder?'

She felt a shiver of fear run through her. 'You will be careful, won't you? Supposing they try to get rid of you too?'

His eyes narrowed thoughtfully. 'I can look after myself. It won't be the first time I've had to deal with this sort of thing. I can play it pretty dirty myself if I have to, but I don't want you involved any further. You can exercise your talent of feeding the brute and keeping me happy. Is it a deal?'

He held out his hand to her and she took it without any hesitation. 'Not everyone likes my cooking. Gloria didn't!' she said with feeling.

'Possibly a recommendation in itself,' he drawled.

She threw back her head and laughed. 'Poor Gloria! I wonder what made her apply for a job out here. I'm sure she'd be much happier back in England!'

'Could be. What about you?'

'Me?' She thought about it. 'I'm happy here. I've never been happier—or, at least, I would be if it weren't for this muddle and my father having to go back to England.' Yet, if her father hadn't gone, Casimir Ruddock would never have come to Isfahan to replace him, and the latter had a lot to do with the warmth of her feelings for Persia and the life she had come to love there.

'Then you don't mind being away from England?'

She was surprised by the question. 'Why should I mind? I've always wanted to travel and see places for myself. I'd like to see America too.' She thought then that she didn't know much about him. She didn't even know which State of the Union was home to him.

'Western Virginia,' he supplied, with that uncanny knack he had for reading her thoughts. 'My family has a farm there. One day it'll be mine and I'll go back there and farm the land, like my father before me. I want my own sons to be born there and to run wild there as I did. We're proud of the life we've made for ourselves there. Even my mother is more Virginian than Polish now.'

'Was she born in Poland?'

'No, but her family came from there. She didn't speak a word of English until she went to school and she still has a slight accent when she gets excited. You'll like her.'

This last was said with such conviction that Stephanie couldn't doubt that he meant it. But what were her chances of ever meeting his mother?

'I'd better go,' she said aloud. 'Thank you for being so nice about everything, Cas.'

He nodded his head, opening the door for her As she passed him, he grinned at her. 'You'd better make it lunch for three,' he said. 'Casimir's dreamboat may come along with me if she hasn't anything better to do.' His grin grew broader. 'Only for lunch, my dear. After lunch, I want to talk to you by yourself, and she'd be decidedly *de trop*! Fortunately, she has an infinite capacity for doing nothing and won't want to come with us if we say we're going out. She's a placid creature despite the somewhat exotic exterior.'

He was plainly devoted to her, a fact that made Stephanie want to say that if he wanted to have lunch with her, he could take her out somewhere, somewhere where she, Stephanie, wouldn't have to watch them together! But how could she tell him that when he was being so kind to her?

She walked to the lift without a backward look, only then remembering that she had left her handbag in her office, nor had she given her bunch of keys to Cas, despite his asking her for them. She turned and looked back at him, and found he was already waiting for her at the door of her office. In silence she preceded him through the door and picked up her handbag and the few personal things she kept in one of the drawers of her desk. When she had done, she thrust the keys into his hand and almost ran back to the lift, pressing the call button with an urgency that made her blood thump in her ears.

Fatemeh took one look at her face as she emerged from the lift on the ground floor and rose from her seat, crossing the room towards her.

'What is the matter, Stephanie? You look as though you have seen a ghost!'

Stephanie took a grip on herself and even managed a smile. 'Mr. Ruddock needs you upstairs,' she said flatly. 'I'm going home.'

'*To England*?'

'Not yet. He—he's coming to lunch. We're going to talk this afternoon. He'll probably tell you about it himself.'

Fatemeh looked first concerned, but then a little spark of humour lit her dark eyes. 'If he is having lunch with you, he won't be sending you back to England! Has there been more trouble about your father?'

Stephanie nodded briefly. 'Someone else *must* have a set of keys,' she whispered. 'Only why should they do such a thing? Whom does it help? That's what I'd like to know!'

But Fatemeh was scarcely listening. 'Stephanie, if you are going to make the lunch yourself you will need someone to go shopping with you. Hold on a minute and I will telephone my home and tell my maid to meet you at your apartment. She can go with you!'

'But can she speak English?' Stephanie objected.

'Of course not, but you can't possibly go shopping by yourself! What are you going to make for lunch?'

Stephanie hadn't the faintest idea. 'Does it matter? All I want to do is to clear up this business here!'

Fatemeh looked amused. 'Mr. Ruddock will do that without your help. I will tell my maid that you are making Kufteh Sabzi for two people, and she must help you, yes?'

'Three people,' Stephanie corrected her. 'He's bringing someone else to lunch.'

Momentarily, Fatemeh looked confused, but she recovered herself quickly. 'Another woman? Is he worried what people will think if he eats alone at your apartment? Who is this other woman?'

Stephanie told her about Amber, trying to keep the open dislike she felt for the other woman out of her voice.

'She dances in public?' Fatemeh repeated. 'Then no doubt she is only a passing distraction and is nothing for you to worry about. She is to chaperon you, nothing more. That much is clear!'

'It would be in Persia—'

Fatemeh patted her hand with real affection. 'Men don't marry their distractions! I expect she is very beautiful, no?'

'Very beautiful!' Stephanie agreed dryly.

'But not the woman to be the mother of his children and to live in his home? That would be too much to believe!'

Stephanie supposed that it would. She didn't see

Amber settling down in the family home in West Virginia somehow, but that didn't stop Cas from being very deeply in love with her, and she said as much. '*Any* man would be flattered to walk into a room with her on his arm!' she added glumly.

Fatemeh shrugged. 'How complicated you make these things!' she sighed. 'I should be worried if my fiancé wanted to show me off to a lot of other men. I much prefer it that he wants to keep me to himself. If he wished to share me with others, how could I be sure of his love?'

How could one ever be sure? Stephanie wondered. She searched in her handbag for her handkerchief and blew her nose. 'Yes, but Cas isn't my fiancé—'

'I'll telephone my maid,' Fatemeh cut her off quickly, so quickly that Stephanie knew that she had some reason to interrupt her. Sure enough when she turned her head, she saw Gloria coming towards them.

'Don't tell me,' the English girl drawled, 'that our busy little bee hasn't any work to do? Has the great man given you the day off?'

'Something like that,' Stephanie managed.

Fatemeh dialled a number and spoke quickly down the phone, giving a series of crisp orders that effectively put an end to the English question and answer session beside her. 'There!' she said when she had finished. 'My maid will meet you as arranged and will take you shopping. Now remember, Kufteh Sabzi. I have already told her all about it. They are little vegetable and meat balls and, I happen to know, they're a great favourite with *him*!' Only then did she acknowledge Gloria's presence. 'Good morning, Miss Lake. How is my brother? Did he tell you that he is leaving for Yazd tomorrow? You will miss him, no doubt, but he will be back for my wedding later on. He will be marrying himself soon. That's why he goes to Yazd, to sign the contract. Her family lives there now, though they used to live close by us in Isfahan.'

'I haven't seen your brother!' Gloria snapped back. 'Unlike some people I could mention, I don't throw myself at every man I meet! But I see your tactics are paying off very nicely where the big boss is concerned!

What favours did he ask in return for the morning off to go shopping? Or is it more than just the morning you're taking off?'

'Much more,' Stephanie answered. 'I'm suspended from working in the office altogether.' She turned on her heel without waiting to see what effect her words had had on the English girl. 'Thank you, Fatemeh, for the loan of your maid. If I get into any difficulties, I'll telephone you to supply the necessary translation.'

Fatemeh giggled. 'Mina will look after you. She is very strict with all of us!'

Stephanie smiled too. 'With Amber too?'

'With you! But she is an excellent cook and she will like to help you. Have a good time, *kouchek*, and find a more cheerful face for your lunch-party, yes?'

'She looks remarkably cheerful to me!' Gloria said unkindly. 'Some people always manage to fall on their feet!' She turned deliberately to Fatemeh. 'Do you *know*—?'

The Persian girl swept up her notebook and pencil. 'I am sorry, Gloria, but I have to go upstairs. Goodbye, Stephanie.'

'How are you going to live if he's sacked you?' Gloria demanded, watching the Iranian girl as she walked across to the lift. 'I thought you'd run home to Daddy! Is *she* going to fill in for you?'

'I think so,' Stephanie answered.

Gloria made a face. 'Why her? I have the seniority. It ought to be me! I think I'll have a little word with our Mr. Ruddock.' Her eyes swept over Stephanie's face without troubling to hide her dislike for her. 'If I were you, I'd watch my step with him! Your father isn't the only person who can be replaced by the company if certain matters come to their ears! And I shall tell him so!'

Stephanie didn't envy her her self-imposed task. 'I should,' she said lightly, and hurried past Ali's desk and out of the building into the sunshine before Gloria Lake could think of anything further to say.

Mina's glum exterior hid a kind heart. Stephanie never discovered whether Fatemeh's orders had covered everything the woman did for her, but she had to admit that she could not have managed without her. In the market, her experience and advice was invaluable, choosing this and that and rejecting the other with brusque efficiency. Afterwards, she sat on the floor in the kitchen and prepared the ingredients ready for cooking. From under her *chador*, she produced a cheap plastic transistor radio which she turned full on, pulling the flap of her veil across her face whenever a man's voice could be heard coming out of the tinny loudspeaker. Later, Stephanie was to find out from Fatemeh that some of the older women still missed the rigid, fitted masks they had worn in their girlhood, but which had been banned in the interests of modernity by the present Shah's father. They felt, so Fatemeh said, much as most western girls would feel if they were obliged to go topless in the streets by government edict. Some of them had spent years immured in their houses rather than face such a humiliation. Some had never gone out ever again, though those mostly belonged to a generation that was fast dying out. Most young girls wore, or did not wear, their *chadors* to suit their own convenience and comfort, as Fatemeh did herself.

Stephanie insisted on setting the table herself. The equipment she had at her disposal was decidedly limited, so she decided to make up for this with colour, using little nosegays of flowers to decorate the table where the side-plates might have been, and yet others to hide the lack of cutlery and the rather ugly glasses that were all she could find.

When she had finished, she found that Mina had laid out a clean dress for her on her bed, having taken the trouble to iron it and to find just the right coloured scarf to wear to set off the neckline. Stephanie was a little surprised at her choice and even tried to question it, but every remark the old man made came back to Fatemeh, and Stephanie came to the conclusion that Fatemeh had been more than explicit in her instructions. Not a single detail had been left to chance.

And it was a very pretty dress. It had a wide collar that stood up behind her neck to reveal her shoulders, and a pleated skirt, the inside of the pleats providing the only colour in what was otherwise a pure white dress. The scarf was of the same sizzling shade of petunia as the pleats. Stephanie enjoyed wearing it and she donned it now with pleasure, studying the picture she made in the glass. With her honey-coloured tan, nearly as deep as her hair, her wide hazel eyes which held a surprisingly happy and expectant expression, and a soft, slightly vulnerable look to her mouth, she thought she was more pretty now than she had ever been in her life before. But then the vision of Amber's striking beauty rose unbidden in her mind and she knew that there could be no comparison between them. Paris would have had to be half blind to award the golden apple to Stephanie in any contest between them!

When the knock came on the door, Stephanie felt overwhelmed by an unaccustomed shyness as she went to open it. Cas was standing there alone and from the appreciative glint in his eyes as he looked her up and down she thought that Fatemeh's choice had been a good one.

'Where's Amber?' she asked him.

'She'll be along. You're looking very striking! I wonder why?'

'To boost my morale,' she told him.

He appreciated that. 'It does mine good too. You look good enough to eat, but then you always look cool and fresh. It's just one of the things I like about you!'

'Oh?' She would have liked to know what the other things were, but she was too shy to ask him. Instead, she was hard put to it not to blush and stammer like a schoolgirl, especially when he ducked his head, ignoring her outheld hand, and kissed her lightly on the cheek. What a pity it was that Amber had to come at all!

'I owe it to her,' said Cas, reading her thoughts as always. 'You don't have to worry about her, you know. Amber's not your enemy.'

Unconvinced, Stephanie thought it wiser to change the subject. 'Beer?' she asked him with a smile.

He shook his head. 'Not today.' His smile told her why not. 'How do you feel about wine? Amber's bringing a couple of bottles of sparkling stuff with her that she's been holding for me in her ice-box.'

Stephanie stiffened. 'You've seen her already today, have you?'

'I had something I wanted her to do for me.' He sniffed the air expectantly. 'Is that going to be as good as it smells?'

'I hope so. I've had the help of Fatemeh's maid all morning. It's her transistor you can hear in the kitchen.'

Cas smiled, enjoying the picture she made. 'Sounds promising.' He sat down, spreading his long legs out before him. 'Where do you want to go this afternoon?'

'It depends,' she murmured. 'My favourite place of all is the Friday Mosque, but if I'm not going to like whatever it is you have to say to me, I'd rather go somewhere else. New Julfa, for instance.'

'The Armenian quarter?' He gave her a quizzical look. 'I think we'll settle for the Friday Mosque.'

She wondered what he would do if she were to argue the toss with him, but her courage died in the face of his quiet determination. 'Has Fatemeh done your letters nicely?' she asked instead.

'We've been too busy to get through much of the routine stuff. She's found a gadget I can dictate into any time I want, though, and she says she'll get the lot typed up for me while I'm out on the road.'

Her spirits fell with a bump. She had forgotten he was going away, and what on earth was she going to do without him?

'Who are you taking with you?' she asked him, her voice shaking despite herself.

The knock at the door came simultaneously with his answer. 'That's one of the things I want to talk about,' he said. He got leisurely to his feet, looking down into her wide, startled eyes. 'Are you going to let Amber in, or shall I?'

'Cas, they'll never let you take *me!*'

'It depends in what capacity I take you.' He went to the door and opened it, putting both arms affectionately round the newcomer's inviting waist and holding her tightly against him. 'Amber, I love you! Hand over the wine and I'll see what I can do about opening it.' His eyes rested on Stephanie for a moment, unexpectedly warm and affectionate. 'You can get the glasses, honey,' he said.

CHAPTER VII

Amber was unashamedly appreciative of good food and she made no secret of the fact that she had come to lunch only because Cas had told her that Stephanie was an extremely good cook.

'You don't mind, Stephanie, but I have always been greedy. Food is the great love of my life—as Cas will tell you!'

Stephanie hid her surprise behind a casual smile. 'I thought singers and dancers were always dieting. Not that you have to worry,' she went on hastily.

'She means,' Cas drawled, 'that you look a million dollars as always!'

'No thanks to me,' Amber said, somewhat smugly. 'All my family are the same. We stay thin until we are thirty and then we look comfortable for the rest of our lives.' She smiled, but at herself, not at them. 'When I am thirty I shall retire and go home. It is not long now!'

'Will you be able to manage?' Cas asked her.

She shrugged. 'Yes, I shall manage. My people look after their own, so we shan't starve. I can hardly wait!'

Stephanie blinked. Who were her people? 'Where is home?' she asked aloud, trying not to sound too curious.

Amber smiled across the table at her, not at all put out. 'I am Armenian. Didn't Cas tell you? I live in the Lebanon, in Beirut, but we have no real home any more. That's why I come to Isfahan often, because of the Armenians who live here. They are not entirely sure that they approve of the way I dance, but they welcome me to their homes, and there is the Cathedral in New Julfa. I like to follow the old customs whenever I can.'

'The Armenian Church is Orthodox, isn't it?' said Stephanie, bringing out the only thing she knew about Armenians, except that they were one of those nations whom all others seem to persecute from time to time. Hadn't they been driven out of Armenia at one time? And the Soviet Union? And Turkey? She was ashamed to think that until this moment their history had really passed her by.

'Yes, Orthodox. But our liturgy and ritual is in our own language. You must visit the Cathedral and see it for yourself.'

'I'd like to,' Stephanie said, and wondered why the other two should exchange glances as though they shared some private joke at her expense.

'What is your religion?' Amber asked her, as though it were the most natural question in the world.

'Church of England—'

'Episcopalian!' Cas exclaimed. 'I thought as much!'

'Does it matter?' Stephanie demanded.

'Not to me, honey. It might have been easier if you had been Catholic, but I'm not complaining.'

'Easier? What's easier about it?'

Amber laughed. 'Didn't he tell you? Cas is a Catholic. What else would he be with a Polish mother? They are all Catholics, I think.'

'We sound like the World Council of Churches.' Stephanie said faintly.

'Don't we just?' Cas agreed. 'But we can all go to Amber's church, which is a very satisfactory answer to the problem.'

'What problem?' said Stephanie.

'I'll tell you later,' he promised. And with that she had to be content. He really was the most maddening person sometimes! He would stop her questions with a remark like that, turning his attention away from her with a decisiveness that made it impossible for her to persevere. It was awesome how easily he managed to get his own way as far as she was concerned!

'Have a little more wine?' he tempted her. 'It's very pleasant, isn't it? Amber's people do most of the wine-growing in Persia. I bought it from some friends of hers this morning.'

'You went to New Julfa?' Stephanie accused him.

He grinned. 'I told you I had a busy morning!'

Amber put her knife and fork together with a sigh of content. 'When I am at home all the time, I shall spend all my time cooking,' she announced. 'I am making my own cookery book, with all my favourite recipes in it. The only trouble is, I never have time to try any of them out. It will be bliss to be in my own home and do it all myself!'

'If last night's meal is anything to go by, I'd say you deserved it,' Cas said forcibly.

'Yes, but this is nice—thanks to Stephanie,' Amber answered him. She picked up her glass and played with the stem, idly turning it round in her exquisite fingers. She looked up suddenly, her eyes deliberately meeting Stephanie's and holding them. 'You mustn't mind that Cas and I are old friends. I did not understand yesterday when he had been cutting your hair, but now he has told me everything and I am pleased. I think he stole more than pieces of hair from you, no? And that is very good. It is time he had someone to make a home for him, and that is good too. But you will not expect him to give up all his old friends, will you?' Her eyes moved away from Stephanie and slid lovingly over Cas. 'We love him too!'

Stephanie didn't need to be told that. She had known it from the first moment she had seen them together. What confused her, though, was that Amber should suppose that *she* meant anything to Cas! Oh yes, he had cut her hair, and he had kissed her too, but he wasn't likely to get further involved with her. He'd be a fool if he did! He had his own career to think about and she knew him to be ambitious, more ambitious, for instance, than her father had ever been. He wasn't the kind to let his heart rule his head! Worse, there were so many to share his heart that if he were to take them seriously, he'd need a harem to keep them all in. What was more, she had a nasty suspicion that while she might gain entry, it would be Amber who would be his acknowledged favourite, and who could be surprised, with her dusky beauty and charming ways?

Cas's hand closed over hers and he poured her out some more wine whether she wanted it or not. 'Drink up, little one! I'm going to make the coffee while you two chatter. It takes an expert to make real coffee and the English in my experience just haven't got the knack!'

She was indignant, as he had known she would be. 'You've never tasted my coffee!'

'Right, so you'll show me what you can do some other time. It's my turn to dazzle you with my accomplishments and, believe me, coffee-making is one of them!

I don't want you to think that I'm helpless when it comes to doing the chores. I was brought up to do my share, let me tell you, and I wouldn't have it any other way!'

'I'm dazzled already,' she said, still grumpy at the high-handed way he had taken over what she considered was her job.

'That's what I'd hoped!' he shot back at her, as imperturbable as ever. 'But I'm happy to have you confirm it!'

Amber laughed her very feminine laugh. 'Cas never lets one have the last word. It's no good arguing with him. He'll do what he wishes to do, so why not let him do it?'

'He doesn't argue, that's the trouble!' Stephanie complained. 'He just concludes that his way is best!'

Amber laughed again. 'Do you want him to argue with you?'

'No, I suppose not.' But Stephanie still felt aggrieved and it showed.

'The wisest woman I know once said to me that I should always suspect a man who allowed me to argue too much with him. Either it would be because he didn't care, or because he was not worth caring about.'

'We look at things differently in the west,' Stephanie insisted, ruffled.

'How dull,' Amber responded, still amused. 'Me, I want to be consulted, sometimes to advise, but to rule —never! If you want that, Cas will only make you unhappy, because he is not the man to allow a woman to run his life for him.'

The idea was laughable! Nor did she want to rule Cas— she knew she would be a fool to try!—but even less did she want Amber's advice on the subject. She could not forget the look that had passed between Amber and Cas and, if it hadn't hurt so much, she would have been horrified to recognise that it was only her jealousy of Amber that prevented her from liking the other woman.

'I think everyone should have a certain measure of independence,' she said austerely. 'Both men and women.'

Amber was as placid as ever, though the glint of laughter stayed in her dark eyes. 'Independence can be too dearly bought. I would give mine up tomorrow, if I could, but it is not yet possible, and I must wait a little longer to be truly happy as I want to be.'

With Cas? Stephanie could hardly bear the thought. She hunched her shoulders miserably, trying not to look at Amber at all.

'Don't you want me to be happy?' the Armenian's soft voice asked her, almost as though she were trying not to laugh.

Yes, but not with Casimir Ruddock! 'Have you ever been to West Virginia?' Stephanie countered.

Amber's eyebrows rose in bewilderment. 'My dear girl, what a question! I'm a city girl! You only have to show me the country for me to wilt. What would I do with myself in a place like West Virginia?'

'Cas's home is there.'

'And mine is in Beirut. That's where my family is. I could never live happily anywhere else!'

Stephanie was glad when Cas came back from the kitchen, carrying three cups of coffee on a tray. She took the cup he handed her and sipped at the brew inside, more than willing to find fault with it. She felt Cas's eyes on her and coloured guiltily.

'Too hot? Too strong? Too bitter?' he taunted her.

She cast him a winning smile. 'Just right!'

His eyes crinkled at the corners, and she blushed in earnest. The mocking look in his bright blue eyes increased her discomfort and she refused to look his way again, afraid of how easily he could completely demoralise her.

To her surprise, Amber rose to go as soon as she had finished her coffee. 'It was a delightful lunch, Stephanie. Thank you for inviting me. You will forgive me, I know, for dashing away, but the afternoon is when I sleep best. At night I am too strung up and it is then that I most hate being away from home.'

Stephanie went with her to the door, and she was even more surprised when Amber gave her a warm hug of farewell, whispering in her ear, 'You do as Cas says, my dear. You're in love with him, aren't you?'

Did the whole world know? First Fatemeh and then Amber—how long would it be before Cas knew too?

'Goodbye, Amber.'

94

'*Au revoir*,' Amber contradicted with a smile. 'We shall surely be seeing each other again. I have my reputation to live up to as Càsimir's dreamboat!'

Stephanie thought she would never forgive Cas for telling her that. 'Do you *like* being called such a thing?' she asked, her eyes wide.

'Of course. I have too few compliments these days. Sometimes I don't feel like a woman at all, but a money-making machine. See you later, honey.'

Bitterly resentful that anyone else should use what she considered to be Cas's own name for her, Stephanie took a deep breath to steady herself before she went back into the room where he was waiting for her. He stood up as she came in, thus robbing her of the advantage of being able to look down on him.

'Thanks, love,' he said. 'Amber doesn't get many treats, but I knew you'd come up trumps with something that would give her pleasure.'

Stephanie found that very difficult to believe, but she said nothing. Instinct warned her that Amber was always going to be a bone of contention between them and that, as she couldn't hide her envy of the other woman, she would do better to pretend to be complacent about her, and she could only do that by ignoring her altogether.

'I'd better clear away,' she said.

He caught her hands in his, cornering her against the edge of the table. 'Mina is going to do that. You, little one, are coming with me! Do you want to take anything with you?'

'My bag—'

'You'd better take a sun-hat and some dark glasses as well,' he commanded her. 'Is this your bag here?'

She accepted her handbag from him and fished her dark glasses out, waving them in front of his nose. 'And I don't need a hat! I can cover my head in the mosque with my scarf. I never wear hats!'

'Don't you? I think you'd look rather fetching in a wide-brimmed straw hat, with a great floppy bow over one eye.'

She looked up at him and felt the rigid control she had kept over the attraction he had for her slipping away from her. She couldn't even remember what it was that

95

he had just said to her.

'Cas, I don't think I want to go after all!'

'My, my,' he teased her, 'I never thought I'd see the well-organised Miss Black looking as scatty as a school-girl on her first date!'

She sniffed reproachfully, hoping that she didn't disgrace herself entirely by bursting into tears. 'Please, Cas,' she whispered.

'You'll be all right with me, Stephanie, and you know it. Surely you trust me enough to see that nothing awful happens to you while I'm looking after you?'

'But I don't know why you should want to look after me?'

He cupped her chin in his hand, making her look up and meet the full force of his blue eyes. 'I'll say one thing for you, honey, you don't suffer from conceit! Don't you know how pretty you are?'

'But not in the same league as Amber—'

'It depends what you're looking for,' he murmured, a muscle pulling at the corner of his mouth. 'In some leagues I reckon you might have the edge even on the luscious Amber!'

'What league?'

'Which league would you like to be top of?'

There was no mistaking the amusement in his voice, or the urgent need she discovered in herself for him to take her seriously. She wanted to be top of his league! Who could possibly want anything else?

'It doesn't matter,' she said. 'I keep telling myself that beauty is only skin deep, but she's nice too, isn't she?'

'Very nice!'

She swallowed, more miserable than ever. 'I think she's in love with you too!' she blurted out.

'If she is, it's a very sisterly affair,' he answered, smiling, and she wondered how it was that men could be so blind in their dealings with women. '*Not* to be taken too seriously, I think!' he added. 'But I've told you that before. You ought to listen more, Stephanie, and jump to conclusions less, but I suspect you're too feminine to do much logical thinking, and I wouldn't really have you any other way!' He patted her cheek and released her, giving a gentle tug to the scarf round her neck. 'This afternoon, honey, the stage is all yours, and you alone will be the leading lady, so you might look as though you're going to enjoy it!'

It was a masterly touch, she thought ruefully, for there was no doubt as to whom the director of the piece was to be. She might be cast as star, but the production would be kept firmly in his own hands—as ever!

'Yes, but, Cas, supposing I don't get my lines right?' she asked in a sudden panic.

'You'll manage,' he said. 'All you have to do is repeat them after me!'

It was too far to walk, he decreed, so they would take a taxi to the Friday Mosque, and what was more he succeeded in finding one with a minimum of trouble, which was slightly unfair when Stephanie thought of the difficulties she had had in getting herself a taxi on innumerable occasions. Either they were of the kind that you shared with other passengers going the same way, and she could never understand where they were going at all, or else they were non-existent whenever they were needed.

Stephanie stepped into the cab first, sliding across the seat to make room for Cas. Her powers of conversation had deserted her and she could think of nothing to say to him at all as they made their way round the huge central square and northwards towards the old part of the town where the Friday Mosque had dominated the surrounding life for a thousand years.

At last inspiration came to her. 'I hope you won't be disappointed,' she said politely, 'the Friday Mosque isn't as colourful as some of the others. But the brickwork is fantastic—and the arches! I find it beautiful.'

'Top of the league?' he suggested.

She nodded. 'But you may not think it as beautiful as the Royal Mosque. Some people don't.'

'What makes you think I haven't the same discernment as yourself?' he asked, tongue in cheek.

She mumbled something, not knowing how to answer him, and was considerably put out when he laughed at her, taking firm possession of her hand that was nearest to him. 'I like colour, but I share some of your passion for order and line too,' he told her. 'It can be more satisfying in the long run—and not only in buildings!'

She didn't know what he meant by that and she was too shy to enquire. She heaved a sigh of relief as they arrived in the rather poor street from which the entrance to the Mosque was visible.

'Over there,' she said vaguely, because she was still turning his last remark over in her mind, 'is the Jewish quarter. The best jewellery shops are there.'

'Is that a hint?' he teased her.

'Certainly not!' she retorted, shocked. But, even so, she couldn't resist a sidelong glance towards one of her favourite shops that stood on the left side of the entrance and was stuffed full of gold and silver objects of every kind, together with a few less valuable ornaments such as a bracelet made from old British halfpennies and one of half-sovereigns that she had looked at long and lovingly only a few days before.

She became aware that he was watching her and hurried through the narrow entrance into the vaulted passage that led the way into the great court of the Mosque. As always the drama of the building built up the excitement within her and her face shone with a personal pride as she felt the big man beside her respond to the beauty of the endless line of arches in a like manner.

The bright sunlight in the main court hit them like a sledge-hammer. Stephanie pulled her hand free of Cas's and arranged her scarf over her head. A crowd of school-girls came surging into the area around them, intent on trying out their few words of English on the foreign visitors. Stephanie would have indulged them if she had been alone, but Cas soon tired of their chatter and led her firmly away towards the *iwan* which covered the entrance into the main prayer hall.

His silence in the face of the enormous domed chamber, flanked by arcades built of bricks in an astonishing variety of pattern, made her look up at him. Only then did she really believe him that he felt as she did about these things. The huge dome towered above them, edged with the praises of Allah written in the picturesque Kufic Arabic script that lent itself so well to the chaste ornamentation that was all that was necessary to complete the marvellous concept of the architect.

'You were right,' he congratulated her. 'A marvellous restorative to put any troubles we might have into their proper perspective. How could one help but feel better in such surroundings?'

'There's another dome on the other side,' Stephanie told him. 'A little smaller, but beautiful too. It was built in 1088, and some people say the mathematics of the stresses and strains were worked out by Omar Khayyám. He's better known in Persia as a mathematician than as a poet.'

Cas was more than willing to follow her round the building, out into the court again and through the western *iwan*, into an enclosed prayer hall-cum-seminary that was entirely lit by alabaster windows. Then into another hall which contained one of the finest *mihrabs* in the world, incredibly intricate and decorative, its original use as a pointer towards the direction of Mecca enhanced by the fantastic ingenuity of its design.

'Where now?' he asked as they came out into the full glare of the sunshine in the paved court.

'You still haven't seen the second dome,' she reminded him.

She took her time wandering through the vaulted arcades on the north side of the building. Standing in ten rows, they were deeper than those on the southern side, but were their rival in complexity of design, leading the eye from one arch to another with satisfying grace.

Stephanie took particular pleasure in showing him the little shrine close beside the smaller dome, where those who had been cured of any diseases which beset them left their mementoes of gratitude, perhaps a leg wrought in silver, perhaps a man in a motor-car who had recovered after smashing himself up in a crash, or perhaps a girl in a surprisingly short, modern skirt whose illness could have been anything. It was so exactly like those similar shrines that exist in so many Mediterranean Catholic churches that she thought it would please Cas too, but he was surprisingly indifferent to the human suffering the shrine represented and contented himself with turning one of the burned-out candles over in the palm of his hand, a strangely watchful expression on his face.

It was comparatively dark, almost gloomy inside the

domed chamber.

'Stephanie,' Cas began, coming up close behind her, 'are you ready to talk?'

She was thrown into confusion. She averted her face, not knowing how to answer him.

'Won't you trust me even now?' he prompted her.

'Oh *yes*!' she exclaimed.

'How much, I wonder? Enough to marry me?'

She turned to face him then, her heart in her mouth. 'Marry you?' she repeated. 'But, Cas—'

'I know it's too soon,' he said. 'Too soon for both of us. But how else am I going to keep you here in Persia? I shan't bother you, or force myself on you, unless you yourself should want it. It would be what they used to call a marriage of convenience, giving me the right as your husband to look after you until we've got everything sorted out.'

She thought it a cold-blooded arrangement. 'I don't know,' she said foolishly. 'I'd have to have time to think about it. I can't believe you really want to marry me!'

He smiled. 'Why should that be so difficult to believe?'

She spread her hands in an expressive gesture. 'You know why! There must be dozens of girls you could marry, Americans like yourself, or—or beautiful and romantic like Amber.' Her voice descended to a whisper on the other girl's name and she bit her lip. 'You don't know *me* at all! I'm—I'm prosaic by nature!'

It was hard to resist the distinct twinkle in his eyes, but she did so nobly, shaking her head at him. 'You can't *want* to marry me!' she insisted.

'I very seldom do anything I don't want to do,' he assured her. 'And as for you being prosaic, you're about as prosaic as that dome up there! A constant and lasting delight to me!'

'You can't know that!'

'Why not?' he countered, his eyes bright and challenging.

'You *know* why not!'

'I don't know anything of the sort! If you really think that I am the wrong man for you, I am, of course, open to being convinced of that. I happen to think that I could make you very happy. I should certainly do my best to do so.'

'But what about *you*?' she asked in a little rush.

'I'm not a boy,' he said. 'I know what I'm doing.'

The temptation was very strong to give way to him then and there. If he had said that he was in love with her, she would have done her best to believe him, because that was what she wanted more than anything else in the world. But he hadn't said anything like that! All he had said was that he wouldn't bother her—a marriage of convenience, he had called it, but convenient for whom?

'Cas, I don't know what to do!'

He was kind as always. 'I know, love, but we haven't time for a long, leisurely courtship. If you hadn't found those letters, or if somebody hadn't brought them forcibly to my notice, you could have gone on working for me as my secretary until you were ready to see me not only as your employer but as a man you wanted to marry. Now, we'll have to get married first and come to terms afterwards. Is that such a bad idea?'

She shook her head. 'But marriage is more than that!'

He put his hand on her shoulder. 'That side of things can wait until you're ready. All I want you to do now is to agree to go through a form of marriage with me so that you can stay on here as my wife. We'll be going on tour almost immediately, where there won't be anyone to ask any awkward questions of either of us. By the time we get back, I hope to have found out more about these letters. We can sort ourselves out when we've got that trouble behind us. Okay?'

She coloured brilliantly and was glad of the gloom all around her. 'Can you wait until then?' she asked him.

'I can try.'

'And what happens if I don't marry you?'

He shrugged. 'I won't have any option but to send you back to England. I'll follow you there as soon as I can, but I have to stay on here until our contract is fulfilled. It will be a long time before I can come to you.'

'But you would come?'

He stood up very straight, looking impregnable and rather intimidating. 'I mean to marry you sooner or later,' he said.

Her throat felt stiff and dry and her voice didn't sound like her own at all. 'Then it may as well be sooner,' she said.

How strange it was, she thought, that something momentous could happen, and yet the world could go on looking just as it had before. The schoolgirls were still crowding together in the central courtyard and the sunshine still blazed down in sharp contrast to the cool, shadowed interior.

Stephanie walked beside Cas, a stranger to herself, someone she didn't know at all, someone so far removed from the orderly person she knew herself to be that she was shocked into silence by her own unnatural behaviour. She, who had always imagined that she would follow the usual logical sequence of meeting some man, getting to know him, falling in love with each other, and only then thinking about getting married, had committed herself to an incredible gamble, that at any other time she would have said was insane, of disrupting the usual order of things, marrying Cas while she could, and hoping against hope that she could persuade him to fall in love with her after the deed was done. She could only conclude that she had gone stark, staring mad! But she couldn't bring herself to regret it! The quivering joy that fountained up inside her whenever she was with Cas rose to a spring tide of happiness that nothing could quench.

'Have you decided you can trust me after all?' Cas asked her as they emerged back into the teeming street.

She managed a rather prim little smile. 'I'm not as fragile as you think,' she told him. 'I—I liked it when you took me to the Khajou Bridge!'

'I liked it too,' he mocked her.

'Well then—' she began.

He grinned at her. 'We'll take it as it comes, little one!' He pushed her fringe back from her brow and she knew he was not entirely displeased. 'If you show me what it was that caught your eye in that shop over there, I might even buy it for you,' he added sardonically. And he bent forward and dropped a quick kiss right on the tip of her nose.

CHAPTER VIII

Stephanie was in her element packing up the Range Rover they were to take on tour with them. It was something that she knew she could do well and she found it a calming experience after all that had happened to her in the last few days. She could almost imagine that she was still the same person she had always known herself to be, except when she caught sight of the gold band on her finger and, with a little jump of the heart, realised that she was not, but somebody very different. She was now Mrs. Casimir Ruddock, sharing that name with a man she hardly knew and who seemed to be more distant every time she set eyes on him.

The strangest part of the whole business was that she had been able to feel nothing at all herself. She hadn't resented the fact that Amber had known all about Cas's plan to marry her before she did herself; she hadn't even minded when she found out that it had been the other girl who had made all the arrangements for the ceremony in the Armenian Cathedral. All Stephanie had had to do was obey the various instructions that everyone combined to give her. If she was asked to give a blood sample, she gave a blood sample, though she hadn't the faintest idea what it was for. All she was told was that it was a necessary preliminary when Americans entered the state of matrimony and that as Cas was an American she had to give a blood sample too. She filled in the forms that were put in front of her, signed her name what seemed like hundreds of times, and came close to having hysterics when Amber tried to coach her in her part of the brief marriage ceremony.

'You'd better write it out for me and I'll learn it by rote,' she had said at last, repentant of the fuss she was making. Even Amber was beginning to look rather frayed, and it couldn't have been easy for her, helping the man she was obviously in love with to marry another girl.

'Oh, Stephanie, I can't! I have never learned to write English! I know only the Armenian script—and the Arabic, of course! You will have to say it after me again and again until it sounds right!'

'I don't think we should be married in church at all!' Stephanie had responded bleakly. 'I can't think why I agreed to go through with this!'

'Because you are in love with him, perhaps!' Amber had snapped, her patience exhausted. 'Is it so difficult to learn a few words that express that love? I should have thought it worth a little trouble to become Cas's wife!'

'You don't understand!'

'Don't I?' Amber had laughed a decidedly brittle laugh. 'Me, I understand very well! You want everything to come from him, all the time! *He* must be loving and understand you, but you can be as temperamental as you like, blowing hot and cold without any thought for how he must be feeling!'

'He doesn't love me!'

Amber gave her a look of pure contempt. 'One does not love a child!'

'But I want—'

'It's a woman that Cas needs. He needs the comfort of a wife, and children of his own. Why don't you think about that? He is hoping you will make a home for him, not a battleground for scoring points because you can't have your own way all the time!'

Stephanie had thought that a bit severe. 'I only want him to love me!' she had protested.

'Be thankful that you can love him,' Amber had advised her. 'You resent it because you think he decides everything for you and you are afraid he will ride roughshod over you, no? But, believe me, there are some of us who would give anything to have their man able to take his place as head of the household and not to have to do everything themselves! It has always been the dream of my life to be able to be myself, and not be the bread-winner and the taxpayer as well!' She had brushed the tears carefully off her long, mascaraed eyelashes with a snowy white handkerchief. 'Never mind, soon I will go home and then everything will be better!'

Stephanie had been busy with her own thoughts. 'Do you think Cas wants children?' she had asked.

'Why don't you ask him?' Amber had retorted. 'You both express the wish to have children in the marriage ceremonial, so it would be well to know before you promise to bear his children, don't you think?'

Stephanie had agreed with her absolutely, but only she knew the impossibility of asking Cas anything of the sort. Their conversation had become increasingly impersonal in the last few days.

Nor had it got any better as their wedding had drawn nearer. It had seemed to Stephanie that one day she had weakly given way to his demand to marry her, and the next they were standing side by side amongst the rather dark pictures that covered the inside walls of the Armenian Cathedral, both of them making their responses in a language that neither of them understood. There had been a dreamlike quality about the whole affair, as though nothing had been quite real, a dream that had taken on a nightmare aspect when they had finally been left alone together.

'How are things going at the office?' she had asked him stiffly.

'Fatemeh seems to be managing quite well.'

'So you haven't missed me at all?' Stephanie had reproached him.

'I didn't say that.' He looked at her for a long moment. 'I haven't had time to do anything very much. I wanted to get a few things settled before we set off on tour.'

Stephanie sighed. He hadn't even kissed her when he had been invited to do so when they had come out of the church. He hadn't so much as touched her all day. She looked up at his stern mouth and wondered what there was about it that she wanted him to notice her so badly, indeed, wanted him to make her blood sing in her veins as he had before. Was he never willingly going to touch her again?

'What sort of things?' she asked in an aggrieved voice.

Cas had opened himself a can of beer and began to drink it, without troubling to find himself a glass. Stephanie's heart sank as she watched him. He could not have made it clearer that he had no intention of kissing her then. If he had, he would have had something else to drink!

'You'd only make yourself miserable worrying about it if you knew,' he had drawled. He had taken another long swig of beer. 'We'll be on the road for four days, honey. Why don't you set about making up a list of the supplies we need and I'll help you stow them away in the Range Rover?'

She had known that all he had wanted was to keep her occupied and out of his hair, but she had been quite unable to resist the challenge of showing how well she could manage such a task, and she had set about it with enthusiasm, enjoying herself for the first time that day.

The Range Rover was already very well equipped. Stephanie had been impressed by the amount of stuff Cas kept by him as a matter of course. There were a couple of sleeping-bags, both of them wider than any she had ever seen before, and both of them very well used. She wondered who had used the second one on previous occasions, knowing even as she did so that she was being foolish to taunt herself by speculating on her new husband's romantic past.

The cooking equipment was far more sophisticated than she had expected as well. There were a couple of burners as well as a grill, which opened up all sorts of possibilities as to what she might be able to cook on it.

'Having fun?' Cas asked her.

She jumped and looked round and to her relief he was no longer looking at her as though he hated her. On the contrary, the amused affection was back in his blue eyes and he was looking as relaxed and as much at his ease as she had ever seen him.

'Is this a company car?' she asked him.

'No, it's my own. I brought it over from the States with me.'

'It's British,' she said with satisfaction.

'I guess I have a penchant for British luxuries.'

'And American know-how?'

'Could be,' he agreed. 'How about you?'

She looked him straight in the face. 'I'm waiting to find out,' she said.

He didn't pretend not to understand her. 'It's something you'd better be sure about before we make a mistake we can't rectify. What's the rush, honey?'

Stephanie turned back to the stove, fiddling with the taps between her fingers. 'I can't think why you married me?' she said.

'But then you're not very sure of yourself at all, are you?' he countered. 'Why don't you concentrate on working out your own motives first? I can wait.'

She was silent for a moment, then she said, 'You don't have to wait because of me. You don't have to treat me like a child.'

'I just think it's something that can easily get out of hand,' he answered wryly. 'I want you very badly, sweetheart, but I don't feel that now is the right time for us. I want it to be perfect for you too, and I don't think it will be while you've got this other business on your mind, and while you're uncertain of me. You haven't been able to forget that I was sent here to replace your father, have you? It must have occurred to you that I might have been behind his going in some way. Me and who else?'

'No!' she exclaimed passionately. 'It isn't true! Oh, Cas, how could you think I could think such a thing of you?'

'Didn't you?'

She could tell that he didn't believe her and she stood up to convince him the better, banging her head on the top of the door. 'I've never doubted you!' she declared angrily.

He put his arms right round her, lifting her down on to the pavement beside him, rubbing her head with surprisingly gentle fingers.

'Then you should have done!'

'Why? You said I could trust you. You *told* me to!'

'Let's hope you're always so obedient,' he teased her. He sounded amused, and more paternal than loverlike.

'I try to keep my promises,' she said to his chest. How much she would have liked to have leaned against him and to have had his arms close round her, shutting out the rest of the world.

'Ah, but did you know what you were promising?'

'Fat chance I had of not knowing!' Stephanie retorted. 'I had Amber coaching me, don't forget! She's a perfectionist, that girl! I don't know how she could, feeling as she does about you!'

He stopped rubbing her head. 'And just what do you

mean by that?'

'You know very well!'

'I wonder if you do,' he said finally. 'Amber doesn't often talk about her affairs.'

'She didn't have to *say* anything!' Stephanie retorted.

'No, she didn't. But she likes you, so she might have said something. Did she?'

'*No!*'

He gave her a quick hug. 'Just enough to make you jealous?'

She was, of course, but that he should know it was too much for her. 'Why should I be jealous?' she demanded. But her voice shook, betraying her, and she hid her face in his shoulder, abandoning herself to the truth. 'She's so beautiful! And I want you to love me!'

She felt his shock as if it had been in her own body. 'Stephanie, are you absolutely sure?' he asked her.

She nodded helplessly. 'I've always wanted it!'

'Look, honey, this is important. I know you're physically attracted to me, but how committed do you want to be?'

She shrugged her shoulders. 'I'm your wife,' she said simply.

He caressed her cheek, pushing her head back to meet his gaze. 'I hope it'll always be enough for you,' he said, and he kissed her very gently full on the mouth.

They finished packing the Range Rover together after that. Stephanie, her mood ebullient, checked off the stores of food on her list and then sat back, watching Cas put it away, marvelling at the easy way he lifted the heavy boxes into the back of the vehicle.

'Were you always big?' she asked him. 'What a Rugby player was lost in you!'

He paused in what he was doing. 'I made out okay in my college football team,' he told her. He grinned reminiscently. 'It was the best way of getting the girls to come around, apart from the glory of being the star of one's class. I liked the girls even better than I liked the team!'

She decided she didn't want to hear about it. 'You would have been safer on the Rugger field,' she said.

'We don't have cheer-leaders and other inessentials to distract us from the really important matter in hand!'

'How often did you play?'

She opened her eyes wide. 'Have you ever seen a Rugby match?'

'Sure,' he said. 'Full of bodily contact, so I was told!'

'Well then, it's a man's game. Women don't play Rugger!'

His mouth twitched. 'Pity,' he murmured.

She giggled. 'Women play Soccer nowadays!' Her eyes glinted with mischief. 'And of course we play all your American games. I played them all at school. Basketball, only we call it netball; and baseball, only we call that rounders. I was very good—'

'It sounds to me as though your experience of playing games has been very limited if those were the only games you played at school,' he drawled.

'Cas!'

'You'd better watch out,' he went on, taking base advantage of her confusion. 'I learned some pretty fancy footwork in my time! You won't escape me easily if I set my mind on having my way with you!'

'How do you know I'm not playing on your team?' she countered.

'So that's the league you're aiming at?' he murmured.

'Oh, Cas, don't tease me! Why else did you marry me? I know I'm not—' She broke off, bitterly aware of what she had been about to say. But there were some things that were better not said, especially to one's husband when one was almost sure that he was in love with somebody else. 'I believe in aiming high!' She caught herself up, lifting her chin to show herself as much as him that she was not afraid of him, or anyone else.

He held out his hand to her, lifting hers to his lips. 'I think we'd better go inside, sweetheart. How will you like to be back in the apartment you shared with your father?'

'I shall miss looking out at the dome of the Madrasseh. It's my favourite of them all.'

His arm about her shoulders was both possessive and disturbing. 'As a married lady you'll have less time to day-dream at your window. What else will you miss?'

'It's never really seemed mine,' she confessed. 'One doesn't get very involved with a hotel bedroom, and it didn't seem much more than that to me. I prefer your apartment. It has a much better cooker.'

'You would know,' he agreed. 'You haven't seen it, though, since you moved out of it, have you? Not until today?'

She shook her head. 'Have you let it get into a terrible mess?'

'You'll have to judge that for yourself!'

She wouldn't have minded if he had. She was besotted enough to have thought it fun to clear up after him. She would have the place clean, tidy, and respectable in a jiffy, and she would enjoy doing it.

But when he opened the door and ushered her inside, it was not chaos that met her eyes, but flowers everywhere and her own suitcases neatly standing within the door.

'I thought you might want to unpack your own things,' he said, 'but you won't need anything right now that I can't supply, will you?'

She couldn't answer him. She had never seen such riches as those banks of flowers. Nobody had ever made such an open-handed gesture to her before!

'Oh, Cas, you shouldn't *splurge*—'

He stopped her mouth with a finger. 'I'll splurge all I like when it comes to my own wife, honey. It would be more gracious to thank me, rather than to stand there adding up the cost, like the housewifely soul that you are!'

'Oh, Cas, I was not!' she denied. 'Only it's too much! A few flowers—'

'Don't you like them?'

'You know I do!' She flung her arms round his neck. 'I wish I were exotic enough to live up to them, but of course I like them!' She touched his cheek with the palm of her hand and reached up to offer him her lips. 'I wish I could have given you something too,' she whispered. 'I didn't even think of getting anything for you!'

'Why should you? It's the man who woos the woman, not the other way round!'

She stared up at him, her eyes dark. 'But I thought—'

'It's too late to ask me to wait now, little Stephanie,' he murmured against her lips. 'You've gone out of your way to convince me it isn't necessary, and I want to know that you're mine. I've wanted to make love to you ever since I bumped into you in the square, and now that you're my wife—'

His lips were soft and warm against hers, but when she made a movement of withdrawal, she realised that he was being deceptively gentle. He had no intention of letting her go. She remembered how easily he had handled her when she had collided with him in the door of the shop, lifting her clear off her feet to prevent her falling, and she knew again the glorious excitement of her own weakness and the longing to submit completely to his male strength.

He picked her up bodily, ignoring her soft protest that she was too heavy for him, and sat down on the easy chair her father had always considered to be his own, holding her closely against him. When he kissed her again, he had forgotten his intention not to frighten her by demanding too much too soon. His lips demanded her compliance and more, leading her quickly to an ecstatic response that she had never known before and which shattered her by its intensity.

'Mmm,' he said. 'You taste nice!'

'So do you.' She smiled shakily, making an instinctive movement to tidy her appearance.

'Not beery?'

She shook her head. 'I wouldn't care if you did!'

He took a pleasure in ruffling her hair and destroying her efforts to smooth down her skirts. 'A sweet disorder in the dress is much more appealing,' he said in her ear. 'Who would have suspected that cool exterior of yours hid such a warm heart?'

She peeped up at him, still shy of revealing her feelings to him. 'I think you did,' she said.

His eyes were incredibly blue. 'Darling, don't ever get hot and bothered about anyone else, will you? I like to think I'm the only one you'll allow to turn your emotions upside down and make chaos of your tidy instincts.'

He did that all too easily! 'I can't help liking things neat!' she protested.

'There's nothing tidy about love, honey. You might as well try to tame a flooding river, or a freak storm, or the waves of the sea. You have to go along with it. If you hold back, it'll wash right over you. It's stronger than you are!'

She ran her fingers through his hair, liking the feel of it. She liked the hardness of the muscles in his shoulders too, and the strength in the arms about her. She strained closer to him. 'You're strong enough for me! Cas, I only want to please you, only I've never—I mean, it's never been like this for me before.' She ran her lips across his cheek and kissed his ear, hiding from the burning light in his eyes. 'I love you!'

His hands found the zip down the back of her dress and slipped inside her bodice, and he smiled against her lips as he felt her heart rocket beneath his touch.

'I'd hate it if you had known *this* before. I want you to be all mine—and you want it too, don't you?'

'You know I do!'

He kissed her again, but more tenderly this time, though she could feel the passion just below the surface, kept firmly under control. She loved him very much in that moment, knowing how easily he could overwhelm her and how little she would have blamed him for doing so, and yet he was giving her all the time she needed to allow her own response to burgeon into life and to blossom into something lovely for them both.

When at last he put her away from him she felt as triumphant as if she had climbed Mount Everest single-handed, and she could hardly contain her glee when she put her hand on his and felt the *frisson* that the contact gave him travel up his arm, and knew with certainty that she could move him, even as he could her.

'What time do we leave in the morning?' she asked him.

'As early as possible,' he answered lazily. 'I thought we'd call by the office first. I want them all to know that we've gone together.'

Her interest was caught. 'Are you up to something?' she demanded.

'Nothing that I plan to tell you about.'

She was hurt and found it hard to hide it from him.

'Something to do with my father?'

'Don't fish, honey. I'm not telling you until I'm good and ready, and that isn't now.'

'I see,' she said. 'I have to trust you, but you don't trust me!'

'That's about the size of it,' he agreed, without interest.

'But why not? I haven't done anything to make you distrust me, have I?'

'I'm not prepared to discuss it!' He rose irritably to his feet. 'Do you want to go out to get something to eat, or shall we have something quietly here?'

'I don't mind.' She felt cold and very close to tears. 'Cas, I would have brought those letters to you sooner or later. I only wanted time to think about it. They were supposed to have been typed by me!'

'Exactly, so drop it, will you?' He made no move to console her. 'How do you feel about caviare and vodka?'

'I'd sooner stay here.' She made a determined effort to put a good face on things. 'If we're going to make an early start I'd like to put my things away and decide what clothes I want to take with me, things like that.'

'Okay.' He bent over her and dropped a kiss on the end of her nose. 'Good girl! You have me to look after you now, but I have to go about it my way. There's too much at stake for both of us!'

'Then you are on my side?'

He grinned. 'Did you doubt it?'

'Not really, but I'm used to fighting my own battles.'

'And your father's too, no doubt. But that's something you gave up when you married me this morning, my love. You're my responsibility now.'

'And my father too?'

'It's all in the family. Don't forget he's now my father-in-law!'

She had forgotten. She was ashamed to think that she hadn't given her family a single thought all day. She had had enough to do coming to terms with her new position as Mrs. Casimir Ruddock. Even so, it was uncharacteristic in the extreme for her to plunge into the unknown without worrying about her parents and the effect it would have on them first and all the time.

'I don't know what they're going to say when they

hear I'm married. I should have sent them a cable. They simply won't believe it!'

'They'll forgive you! When we get back to Isfahan, we'll put in a call and you can speak to them person-to-person.'

'But they don't know you!'

'They will one day. I'm not asking you to give up your family, but I intend to come first with my wife. You'll find it a little different meeting them as my wife and not as just their loving daughter. But different doesn't mean worse! I think you may all come to prefer it.'

'I hope so,' she said, unable to conceal her doubts about that. 'I'm afraid they'll be very angry!'

'If they are, it will be with me.' His smile was warm and affectionate. 'In a few weeks time, when you've got used to things, you'll wonder what you were worrying about. You have remarkably little confidence in yourself, my love, for one who can bring the most difficult of us round her thumb with a flick of the wrist!'

She was astonished that he should think so. And when she thought how much she would like to have her own way with him at times, she thought it unkind in him to tease her about it. 'That'll be the day!' she said on a sigh.

He looked at her with some amusement. 'You'll do!' he assured her. 'You want too much too quickly, but you'll get there in the end.'

She could only hope he was right. And whether he was or not, she would be far better off doing something positive instead of worrying herself to death about it, so she made herself take her suitcases to her room and unpacked them with a fierce concentration which she took on with her into the kitchen, rearranging that too to her complete satisfaction.

By the time she had finished she felt considerably better. When Cas came and stood in the doorway, she smiled at him over her shoulder, glad to see him.

'If you want to eat caviare, we could eat it at home,' she suggested. 'I can easily make us some of those little pancakes, and melt some butter. We even have some cream.'

'Sounds fine to me,' he agreed. 'Can I help?'

She allowed him to set the table when he seemed determined to do something. It still felt odd to her to have a man prepared to help her in the kitchen and she was shy of making too much use of him at first. When he offered to make the batter for the pancakes, she had no excuse ready to prevent him, and found herself standing around watching him for a change and, she had to admit, enjoying the picture he made as he beat the batter into the frothy mixture he wanted.

'Are you going to make the pancakes, or am I?' he asked her.

She put on the pan to heat and reached into the refrigerator for the small jar of caviare that Fatemeh had given them earlier in the day.

'I'll cook them and you can eat them,' she laughed at him.

'Indeed you won't! There's a gadget here to keep the pancakes hot. Cook enough for both of us and we'll eat them together!'

Nothing loth, she put a little of the mixture in the hot pan and tossed it over with the quick, jerky movement she had learned years before.

She heard the telephone ring, but she didn't give it a thought, so intent was she on what she was doing. Cas went to answer it, and she could hear his deep voice arguing with whoever it was at the other end. Then there was a long silence. She didn't even look up when he came back into the kitchen.

'Who was it?' she asked.

'Amber. I'm sorry, honey, but I'll have to go to her. I asked her to do something for me and it's come off sooner than either of us expected.' He kissed her lightly on her warm cheek and tweaked her fringe with his hand. 'I shan't be any longer than I can help.'

'But, Cas, you can't go now!'

His hand cupped her chin and he kissed her again. 'I'll make it up to you, I promise you,' he said gruffly, 'but I have to go!'

She didn't believe him. It would always be the same, she thought. Amber would beckon and he would go running to her, without a thought for the wife he left behind him. She heard him slam the door as he went out without moving her muscle. The tears came slowly, running down her cheeks and hissing as they hit the hot pan below, but she made no move to wipe them away. It was a long time later before she turned off the flame and, leaving everything exactly as it was, went into the bedroom that had been her own when she and her father had shared the apartment before and, as systematically as she did everything else, went through her usual routine before going to bed, only then allowing herself the luxury of crying herself to sleep.

CHAPTER IX

Stephanie lay very still when she heard the front door opening and knew that Cas had returned. She didn't have to look at her watch to know that it was very late. What a way to spend her wedding night!

He went first into the kitchen. Stephanie wished she had taken the trouble to put everything away before she had come to bed. He would know how much he had hurt her when he saw that she had eaten nothing and had not even bothered to wash up the tools they had used together, or to put away the ingredients they had needed for the pancakes.

After a while she wondered what he was doing, but then she heard him coming towards her bedroom door and she lay very still, pretending to be asleep. He opened the door and put his head round, checking to see that she was there.

'Stephanie!'

She didn't answer. It was too late for him to win her round with a few well-chosen words. Did he think she didn't *know* where he had been?

He came over to the bed and sat down on the edge of it, looking down at her in the darkness. She shut her eyes so tightly that they ached and clenched her fists beneath the bedclothes. She would not give in to him now, she would not! She wished she had drawn the curtains to keep out the moonlight, but she liked to sleep with them drawn back, to watch the clouds scudding across the moonlit sky, or to count the stars as they twinkled against a black velvet backdrop. Only now the moon was shining full on her face and she knew that he could see her almost as clearly as if it had been daylight. She felt very naked and vulnerable before his gaze.

He eased the bedclothes over her shoulders and pushed her hair back from her face. 'Tears, Stephanie? I might have known that you'd take it personally, but I had to go, honey. It was important that it should all be set up tonight!'

And she wasn't important? She screwed her eyes up

more tightly and willed herself not to let loose the whimper that threatened to betray her wakefulness. His hand found the nape of her neck and tightened round it, giving her an angry little shake.

'I've a damned good mind to carry you off to my bed whether you want it or not! You're no more asleep than I am, and if you're feeling miserable, it's your own fault for having so little faith in me! Now, are you going to sit up and discuss it like a civilised human being, or not?'

'*Not!*' It came out like an explosion and she turned her face into her pillow, no longer making any effort to hide the sobs that shook her.

'Why not?' His voice was tough and austere and sounded as though he meant to have an answer.

'You know why not!' By contrast, she thought she sounded timid and unsure of herself, and she thought how extremely unfair it was that being in the right didn't help her at all when it came to taking up arms against him.

'Do I?' he said grimly. 'As your grievance is entirely in your own imagination, how can I possibly know what you've dreamed up to make yourself miserable about? Okay, neither of us wanted me to have to go out tonight, but I hadn't any choice, so what do you expect me to do about it?'

'Nothing.'

'Nothing?' He reached forward and turned on the bedside light, taking in her tear-stained face without comment. 'I guess you don't know me very well if you think I'm the kind of man who gives way to his wife's moods. If you want to throw a tantrum, go ahead and throw it, but don't expect me to go round walking on eggshells to keep you sweet. I won't do it!'

'It's not a mood!' she protested. 'I was tired and I came to bed, and I want to be left *alone!*'

'And what about what I want?'

She licked her lips, a little afraid of him. 'It's late,' she pointed out on a quavering note. 'And we have to make an early start tomorrow.'

'True. Was that any reason not to share my bed?'

She tried not to look at him, pleating the edge of the sheet between her fingers and then pulling it out straight again. 'I changed my mind,' she whispered. 'You said you wouldn't—not until I was ready—'

'You're ready!' he retorted. 'I wish I could get it out of my head that you're trying to teach me a lesson. Are you, Stephanie?'

She shook her head. 'It's just that everything happened so quickly!' she blurted out. 'I need time to catch up with myself! Is that so much to ask?' She still avoided his eyes, humiliated that she couldn't bring herself to face him with the truth. Surely, any wife would be within her rights to resent her husband rushing off to be with another woman on their wedding night. She wasn't being unreasonable by refusing to welcome him back with open arms! 'Please, Cas,' she added on a note that made her burn with shame at her craven self, 'don't be angry with me!'

'If I'm angry, it's because I wanted you to be happy,' he said with wry self-mockery. 'And I think I could make you happy too, but I've never taken a woman yet without her consent and I'm not going to start with my wife!' He switched off the light and then switched it on again. 'But I don't see why I should deny myself the privilege of kissing you goodnight, do you?'

She gave him a prickly look, tensing up, and somehow managing to look very young and insecure. 'I can't stop you,' she said.

He put his hands underneath her pillows, lifting them and her into his arms. For a long moment he looked deep into her clouded eyes and then he covered her mouth with his, parting her lips with a masterful ease that made a nonsense of her determination to stand out against him. Her heart quickened within her, beating in unison with his, and she found it more and more difficult not to give him the response he was seeking. She withstood the first kiss, but his seeking hands undermined her concentration, turning her body into a traitor to her cause and, at the second kiss, she made no effort to resist him at all, clinging to him and kissing him back with all the fervour of which she was capable.

He released her gently, tracing the outline of her mouth with his finger. 'I hadn't intended it as such,' he murmured, 'but let that be a lesson to you, my darling. There's such a thing as cutting off your nose to spite your face.'

Her mouth felt dry with shock. 'What do you mean?'

'Think about it!' he advised her. He bent forward and kissed her anxious eyes, snapping out the light at the same moment. 'Perhaps your need is greater than mine. If I'm prepared to accept you as you are, can't you do the same for me?'

Taking second place to Amber, she supposed. Her mind revolted at the thought, but she had to admit that her body wasn't prepared to be so particular. It was becoming increasingly hard to deny the strong physical attraction that lay between them, and she had to remind herself again and again that that could never be enough for her.

'I do have some pride,' she sniffed.

'What as? As a woman? As a wife?'

'As a *person*,' she insisted.

'Great! That'll really set you up in life!'

His contempt seared her spirits. 'It's better than having no pride at all! One can't grasp at everything that comes one's way because it looks attractive at that particular moment. There's more to life than candyfloss!'

His features relaxed into a smile. 'Untidy stuff, candyfloss,' he observed. 'Still, it's easier to put in its place than husbands!'

She was so relieved that he was back to normal that her courage surged back into her. 'Or wives either!' she retorted.

'But then I can stand a bit of clutter,' he answered her. 'I'll never want to put you away on the shelf and dust you down every now and then—'

'I wouldn't do that to you either!' she exclaimed.

'I just thought I'd warn you against it in case it should ever cross your mind,' he said dryly. 'I intend to be a great deal more than an ornament in your life. Understand?'

She blinked, rather less sure of herself. 'Cas, I want to know you better before—'

'No, you don't, honey. We both know what you want, but, just for tonight, we'll play it your way and I'll leave you alone to work things out by yourself. I'm not sure I'm doing you much of a favour, but I'm tired too and in no mood for long preliminaries either. We'd better get some sleep. Goodnight, Stephanie.'

She knew she wouldn't sleep a wink if he left her now. 'I won't feel any different tomorrow!' She cast him a swift look through her eyelashes. 'I'll still want more time!'

'Goodnight, Stephanie!'

'Don't you care?' she shot at him.

'Not much. Tomorrow we're going to do things my way, however much time you think you want—or claim you do! That'll give you something to dream about tonight!'

His arrogance took her breath away. Her mouth fell open and she stared up at him. 'Even if—if I hate you?'

'You'll have to persuade me of that first, and you'll have quite a job to do that. What you need, young lady, is a firm hand, and I'm just the man to give it to you! Who has a better right than your husband?'

'Cas—'

'Goodnight, Stephanie.'

'Goodnight, Cas,' she answered meekly. She sat up, hugging her knees through the bedding, wanting she knew not what. 'I'm sorry,' she added.

He ran his fingers through her hair, rubbing her scalp with a friendly hand. 'Sleep well, sweetheart. Tomorrow is another day, and it'll all be there waiting for us. I'm sorry too. Sorry I had to go out and leave you on your own, and sorry that I haven't yet gained your trust sufficiently for you to know that I'd never willingly hurt you.' He bent his head and kissed her cheek, preventing her from smoothing down her hair by the simple expedient of catching her hand in his. 'What a pretty little thing you are!'

She was inordinately pleased that he should think so, even if it wasn't altogether true. Beside Amber, she knew she looked ordinary and colourless, but it didn't stop her wanting to be beautiful to him. She reached up and returned his kiss, giving him a quick hug as she did so. And then he was gone and she was left with only the memory of his tall form leaning over her and the feel of his lips on hers. Tomorrow, she repeated to herself like a charm; tomorrow, and tomorrow, and tomorrow!

Rather to her surprise, Stephanie went to sleep almost immediately and the sun was already high in the sky when she opened her eyes and thought with joy that this was the day that she was going on tour with Cas.

The memory of how she had left the kitchen brought her swiftly out of bed and, throwing on her bathrobe, she crept through the flat in an agony lest she should awaken her husband before she was ready for him. The kitchen was every bit as bad as she remembered it to be, but the sight of the caviare and the pancakes she had made the night before aroused her appetite and she began to feel quite hungry. The mixture was probably all the better for having been allowed to stand overnight, and after only a moment's hesitation she lit the light under the heavy iron pan and set about making more pancakes for their breakfast.

She had barely finished when she heard a thud in the living room.

'Cas?'

He appeared, yawning, in the doorway. He looked different for a moment and then she realised it was because he hadn't shaved. She could hardly take her eyes off the shadow round his chin. She wondered what it would feel like against her face and coloured in case he should guess what she was thinking.

His eyes were the same, though—very blue and full of laughter. 'Some breakfast!' he teased her.

'The caviare might not keep,' she defended herself. 'I've left the coffee for you to make, if—if you don't mind?'

'A fair division of labour!' He helped himself to a pancake, poured some hot butter on to it, smothered it with caviare, and topped the lot off with some cream. 'Some breakfast!' he said again.

Cas made the coffee with a minimum of effort, watching at the same time the neat way she served herself with the pancakes, cutting them into four equal pieces and transferring the quarters systematically to her mouth.

'Try one with a blob of cream,' he recommended.

She did so, guessing by his smile that he was waiting for her to make a mess of it and drop it down her front. When she had successfully eaten two pancakes smothered in caviare and cream without accident, she allowed herself a brief look of triumph in his direction and was surprised by the loving gleam in his blue eyes. She put her spoon and fork down on her plate with a little clatter and, breathing rather more heavily than usual, she collected up the dirty dishes and plunged them into the sink, turning on the taps as she did so. The water shot into the plastic bowl, hit one of the plates and showered upwards into her face.

'Oh, damn!' she said.

Cas put his hands on her shoulders, turned her round to face him, and mopped her up with a handy tea-towel. He was trying hard not to laugh at her, but she could feel it in the tremor in his hands. He was so close to her and yet so far away!

'What a pity we have to go,' he said.

Her heart missed a beat and then raced like a mad thing within her. Perhaps he wasn't as far away as she had thought. She brushed down the front of her shirt with her hands, her expression one of delicate distaste as she felt the dampness that the water had left. And then she could bear the space between them no longer. She turned into his arms, flinging her own about his neck.

'Oh, Cas, you haven't shaved and you feel horrid!'

'Scratchy,' he agreed solemnly. 'You don't fancy me with a beard?'

She fancied him any way at all. 'If it grows quickly,' she murmured against his neck. 'I don't want to have permanent gravel rash!'

He held her away from him, looking down at her, his eyebrows raised. 'Is there any danger of that?'

She bit her lip. She had pleaded with him that she wanted time and now he was forcing her to admit to herself, even more than to him, that that had been an excuse to cover the jealousy she felt for Amber.

'I want to come first—'

'Honey, I married you. Isn't that enough for you?'

She nodded, her eyes bright with unshed tears. 'But

I'd sooner you shaved before you kissed me again,' she tried to joke.

'I'll bear it in mind,' he drawled. 'Are you packed and ready to go? Because if so, I'll leave you to finish up in here while I get my own things together.'

Stephanie was conscientious about leaving the apartment as she wanted to find it. There was not a thing left out of place. She even swilled out the drying-up cloths and left them spread over the draining board to dry. She was particular, too, about the few garments she was taking with her, folding them with inordinate care so that they wouldn't crush in the suitcase.

Cas, she noticed, had a totally different method of packing. He gathered everything he thought he would need in a pile on his bed, and then stuffed it bodily into the bag he had at his feet, zipping it shut with impatient fingers. In future, Stephanie decided, she would do his packing for him. Yet she hadn't noticed that he went round in crushed shirts and baggy trousers, so perhaps there was more method in his system than she had allowed for. Perhaps he looked more careless than he actually was.

He picked up both cases and carried them out to the waiting Range Rover. Stephanie locked and checked the door, following him out more slowly, clasping the keys in her hand ready to give them back to him. But when she approached the Range Rover, she saw that there was a third person included on the trip, a young Iranian in a Chinese-looking hat, who was already installed behind the wheel of the vehicle.

'This is Idries,' Cas introduced them. 'He's coming along to translate for me and to share the driving. Idries, this is my wife.'

The young man didn't quite look her in the face, but he held out his hand to her and smiled, showing very white teeth against the brown tan of his skin.

'I drove your father sometimes, *madame*,' he said.

She looked at him more closely, but she didn't recognise him as being one of the drivers her father had usually used. However, she smiled back at him and tried to look pleased that he knew who she was.

She made a move towards the Range Rover, meaning

to give Cas the window seat, but he was before her, sitting firmly between her and Idries.

'But you need the extra room for your feet,' she murmured uncomfortably.

He grinned at her. 'I can always spread them out a little in your direction. You can sit in the centre seat when I'm driving.'

She gave him an uncertain smile, a little surprised by his attitude. She got in beside him and studied her hands with an interest she was far from feeling while she made up her mind if it was Idries's driving he didn't trust, or if he thought she would encourage the young man to be more familiar than he liked. The possibility that he might be a little jealous of her was new to her and she hugged the thought to her, hoping that she wasn't deceiving herself.

'I'd hardly flirt with Idries in front of you,' she said, feeling her way carefully in case she had got it all wrong and he wasn't jealous of her at all.

'It's better to be sure than sorry,' he retorted dryly. 'You've got your hands full relating to me just now. That's excitement enough for you until you can bring yourself to trust me a little bit more than you do now.'

She opened her eyes very wide. 'Don't you trust me?' she asked him.

'Can I?'

The bubble of mirth in her middle died away. 'Yes,' she said.

'I hope so. An awful lot depends on it.' He ran his finger down her nose, smiling. 'But you never know with a woman,' he teased her. 'They can't resist trying out their skills on anyone handy, and Idries looks the susceptible type!'

'I've never heard them described as skills before,' Stephanie muttered, anxious not to sound as stuffy as she felt. 'And if you must know, I'm not given to flirting at all!'

He looked amused. 'Ah, but it's when one has discovered a new skill that one most wants to try it out!' he mocked her. 'If you're wise, little one, you'll restrict yourself to experimenting with me. Is it a bargain?'

She frowned at him thoughtfully. 'What a funny idea

you have about women!'

His smile flashed out. 'Haven't I, though? But I think I understand them well enough to be able to handle my wife without any help from outsiders, male or female. As you'll find out, if you cross me too often!'

She wasn't sure if he was serious or not, but she thought it safer not to find out. She sat up very straight in her seat, staring out of the window at the busy street scene outside.

'Where are we going?' she asked as Idries started up the engine.

'I have to call by the office first—'

'Good. I'll come in too. I want to thank Fatemeh—'

'No, love, I'd prefer you to wait outside. I'll send Fatemeh outside to have a gossip with you in the car. Tell her you want to buy some *gaz* for the journey, you may be glad to have something to suck during the heat of the day.'

'I thought *gaz* was like butane, something one cooked on?'

'Not in Isfahan. Here it's a kind of nougat with pistachio nuts in it. It's good—not too sweet!' He felt in his pocket and pulled out a handful of notes, some of which he pressed into her hand. 'Get yourself a box of the stuff, and give Fatemeh some too!'

'But I have enough money!' she protested.

'Husband's privilege,' he retorted with a sidelong grin. 'Put it in your pocket, Stephanie, and let me enjoy treating you. I haven't had the opportunity to buy you much so far, and a few sweets won't bankrupt me.'

Her fingers closed over the notes. He had given her a ridiculous amount for a few sweets and they both knew it. 'Thank you, Cas. I'd like to give Fatemeh something. It was her caviare we had for breakfast.' She lowered her lashes so that she didn't have to meet his eyes. 'What are we going to give her when she gets married? I'd like to get her something really English, but I don't want you to feel left out.'

'She's your friend, honey. What had you thought of getting her?'

She took a deep breath. 'A cashmere twin-set. I could get my mother to send it out here, but they're not cheap to begin with, and there's bound to be a whole lot of duty. Would it be too much?'

He wiped all trace of expression off his face. 'Are you asking me to pay?' he asked.

She nodded, still not looking at him. 'I haven't got that kind of money,' she confessed. 'But I can think of something else, if you—if you think it's too much?'

He leaned back against the back of the seat, a smile of pure content breaking over his features. 'I had a bet with myself that the first thing you asked me for would be something for your parents, the second something for a friend, and then possibly something for yourself! I wasn't too far out, was I?'

'I don't want to impose,' she said quickly. 'I'll put something towards it too. But I thought you might like—'

'And so I do!' he assured her. 'I like it very much! I shall like it even more when you ask me for something for yourself!'

'You gave me the flowers,' she reminded him.

'That was just the beginning.' He chuckled at the look on her face. 'I've never had a wife of my own to give things to before and I mean to make the most of it! Some really gay little dresses, for instance, that *nobody* would wear in the office. They'll go with your fringe.'

'Oh, but something quieter would be more useful.' He had to be teasing her, of course, but it would be fun to buy a few things just because they were pretty and not with an eye as to their suitability and whether they were strongly enough made to last two seasons rather than one. 'Cas, you shouldn't spoil me. I might get to expect it, and I can't bear people who aren't grateful when they're given things!'

He patted her knee, leaning forward as they drew up outside the office building. 'I don't think there's any danger of that,' he said.

Stephanie got out of the Range Rover and walked up and down the pavement after he had gone inside. She would be sitting for long enough once they got going not to take advantage of every stop they made. She went up to the glass doors of the building and smiled at Ali through them. She saw Fatemeh coming out of the lift, pulling her *chador* about her shoulders as she came. And behind her there was another woman, a woman she would have recognised anywhere, the woman who haunted her dreams and turned them into nightmares. It was Amber. But what was she doing there?

She put up a hand to push open the door, but changed her mind as Fatemeh came hurrying out to her.

'Was that Amber who came down with you in the lift?' she demanded in a high, unnatural voice. 'What's she doing here?'

Fatemeh gave her a compassionate look. 'She had something to say to Mr. Ruddock.'

'Again?' Stephanie sighed.

Fatemeh plucked at her *chador*. 'It's better to pretend you haven't seen her.' Satisfied that her veil was now to her satisfaction, she turned her full attention on her friend. 'Mr. Ruddock said you had some shopping to do. What is it you wish to buy?'

'Some *gaz*. He said to get some for you too.' Stephanie allowed herself to be propelled down the street towards a little row of shops at the corner. 'Does she come to the office often since—since I've been gone?'

'They have business together,' Fatemeh answered reluctantly.

'What business?'

'If Mr. Ruddock wishes you to know, he will tell you himself. I can't tell you, Stephanie! All I know is that you are not to go inside—'

'Because he doesn't want me to see her!'

'Perhaps,' the Persian girl admitted.

'He saw her last night too! Fatemeh, what am I going to do?'

Fatemeh put her hand on her arm, turning her round to face her. 'You must not do anything. You don't know why they are seeing each other and if you guess, and guess wrong, what will you say to Mr. Ruddock then? She is an old friend of your husband, but you are his wife. Do you think Mr. Ruddock would forget that?'

Stephanie blinked. 'He might not be able to help it. She's so beautiful! And I'm not! I'm not even passable. She makes me feel stiff and awkward and—and *gauche*! I don't know why, because I don't hold my petticoat together with safety-pins and I'm sure she does. But it doesn't seem to matter with her!'

Fatemeh uttered a short, squeaky laugh. 'Perhaps it is too important to you. Though I expect when Amber is home with her husband she relies less on pins and more on her needle—'

'Her husband?'

Fatemeh jerked to a halt. 'But I thought you knew, Stephanie, that she was married? It is only recently that she has come here by herself. Before, they always came together. They used to work together. He was even more famous than she as a dancer. But this year and last year she came alone. There was a rumour that he had divorced her, but this was denied by her manager in all the local papers. It's not as easy for Armenians to divorce as it is amongst us, but she is always talking about going home, so I think she must still be happily married.'

'Does Cas know her husband too?' Stephanie asked in a frozen voice.

Fatemeh shrugged. 'You must ask him that. How would I know? But you would do better to put her out of your mind and work at pleasing your husband instead. If he had seen any future for himself with Amber, he would not have married you!'

'But he couldn't marry her if she's married to someone else,' Stephanie pointed out. But why had he married her? Because he had guessed the way she felt about him and had felt sorry for her?

Fatemeh pulled her veil across her face as they reached the shop they were going into. 'Perhaps that is why he married you,' she said carefully as though she was searching for the right English words that would convey her exact meaning. 'But, Stephanie, who will you help if you make him regret marrying you? Be happy that he wanted to make you his wife. You will still be beside him long after Amber has gone back to Beirut and her husband. Me, I find your position more enviable than hers! You have years in which to be loved by him. What has Amber had?'

Stephanie didn't know. She knew that she had stolen her wedding night and that she was there, talking to Cas at that very moment, when she herself was forbidden even to go into the office building. And she knew that she could never see Amber without wondering just what she had meant to Cas—what they still did mean to each other.

She followed Fatemeh into the shop and paid for the two gaudy boxes of *gaz*, hardly looking at them as she tucked her own box under her arm and gave the other one to the Iranian girl.

'I love him so much!' she said as they came out into the street again.

'Then make him happy by telling him so,' Fatemeh responded gently. 'Tell him so often, Stephanie, and make yourself happy too!'

CHAPTER X

Cas seemed twice life size as he came through the glass doors. It made Stephanie catch her breath to see him—he was always at least three inches bigger than she had remembered him to be.

'What's Amber doing here?' she demanded.

His only answer was to laugh at her. 'You're jealous!' he accused her. He whirled her right off her feet, holding her high above his head, as if she were no more than a child.

'Cas!' she exclaimed. 'Cas, put me down!'

She wouldn't have put it past him to toss her right up into the air and she clutched at him to prevent the indignity, trying to tuck her shirt more firmly into her trousers at the same time. He held her close and rumpled her hair.

'Love me?' he asked her.

She found herself looking straight into his eyes, for once on the same level as himself. The street vanished from her consciousness, all thought of Amber forgotten. She didn't even care that her shirt had parted company with her trousers altogether.

'Yes.'

He put her gently back on to her feet. 'Good,' he said. The street came back into vision and Stephanie blushed to the roots of her hair. Fatemeh was looking at her askance, her eyes bright with laughter.

'What's so funny?' Stephanie asked her in a fierce aside, valiantly trying to restore order to her usually neat appearance.

Fatemeh murmured something in her own tongue, drawing the flap of her veil more closely across her face. 'I am his witness,' she added in English, still giggling.

Stephanie could have stamped her foot in rage. She hated to be made to feel foolish at any time, but to treat her like a child in public was something she would find it hard to forgive the large man at her side.

'I hope you're satisfied?' she glared up at him.

His laughter could have been heard half-way down

the street. 'For now,' he answered her. 'Things are going very well indeed! Come on, love, we'd better be going.' He held out his hand to Fatemeh. 'I guess you know what you have to do, Miss Ma'aruf? Don't forget to lock everything up when you leave. It's all set up.'

Fatemeh nodded. She glanced briefly at Stephanie and then back at the American. 'I will do exactly as you told me. No one but myself will go into your office, or into Stephanie's either.'

Cas's lips twitched. 'Except that it's your office now,' he reminded her.

'For a little while.' The amusement came back into her eyes. 'Or is your wife to lead a life of leisure now that she is married to you?'

He didn't seem to resent the question. 'Could be,' he said. 'How about you, Miss Ma'aruf? Are you going on working after you're married?'

Fatemeh shook her head, looking embarrassed. 'My family is very modern, but not that modern. Persian women prefer to stay at home and look after their families. They have great influence with their husbands and sons, but they don't like to be seen often in public. Me, I am very Persian!'

'Yet your family allowed you to work,' Stephanie put in. 'Wasn't that a great step forward?'

Fatemeh shrugged. 'It has been interesting,' she admitted. 'I wanted to be able to talk to my future husband about the things that interest him and now that I know something of his world, I can do this. But I prefer to keep to my own sphere after my marriage.'

'Quite right!' Cas commended her. 'See what you can do about persuading Stephanie that I come first, will you? You could even teach her to wear a *chador* and I shouldn't object!'

Stephanie sighed. 'He's afraid I'm going to run off with the driver, Idries!'

Fatemeh was not amused. 'Stephanie! How can you joke—'

It was Cas who came to his wife's defence. 'Stephanie has never lacked courage,' he drawled. 'Least of all in her dealings with me.'

Yet there had been times when she had been more than

a little afraid of him, but that was her own secret. Sometimes it was the most exciting thing in the world, like just now, when he had swept her off her feet and had tossed her up in the air. She could protest all she liked that she didn't like to be handled and that she liked to keep her feet firmly on the ground, but she couldn't deny the ecstasy that fired her blood when he destroyed her reserve with his superior strength, and forced her to rely on him rather than on her own, much vaunted, dignity.

'Sometimes I don't feel very courageous,' she said, more to herself than to anyone else. 'I'm not very *anything*!' she added on a note of passion.

'You'll do,' Cas told her. He ordered Idries into the passenger-seat and swung Stephanie up into the Range Rover, settling her into the middle seat and then getting in beside her. 'You'll do me any time!'

It was a long way to where the teams were actually working, setting up the new telecommunications equipment. If Stephanie had ever doubted that Persia was a large country, that day's drive would have convinced her. Mile after mile, they sped across the open, dun-coloured plains, reaching the pass over the mountains, only to find another plain before them, the mirror image of the one before. The dry atmosphere made it possible to see for miles in any direction, the view only restricted by the endless range of mountains that constantly changed colour as the rays of the sun played on their slopes.

After the first hour conversation became desultory and finally died away altogether. Stephanie became increasingly conscious of the stiffness of her limbs and she wished desperately that she and Cas had been alone in the Range Rover, without the constraint of a third person.

'Tired, honey?' he asked her, when a second and then a third hour had slipped by.

She was too proud to admit that she was. 'Not a bit!' She threw him a cautious glance from beneath her lashes. 'How much further do we have to go?'

'We'll stop at one of the Government Rest Houses for lunch. It's not too far now, is it, Idries?'

'No, *aga*, not far now. The very next town. Then we have very nice meal. Madame will feel better then.'

'I feel fine now!' Stephanie declared with more spirit than truth.

'Prepared for anything?' Cas teased her. 'You'll need to be tonight. There's not much chance of our finding a hotel in the middle of nowhere.'

'We have our sleeping-bags.' That reminded her about the well-used state of the two of them. 'You must have slept out often before,' she said. 'Who used the other one?'

'Still jealous?' he mocked her.

'Of course not. I can't imagine—' She broke off, horrified by what she had been about to say; that she couldn't imagine *Amber camping with anyone*!

'My brother and I do a lot of fishing back home,' he answered her original query. 'One of the bags is his. I don't say that no one else has ever used it, but you're the first female, so far as I know. Satisfied?'

'I suppose so,' she murmured.

'What else do you want to know?'

There were so many things. She wanted to know everything about him; ridiculous things like what he had looked like as a small boy, and what sort of things made him laugh.

'I didn't know you had a brother,' she said.

'I have a brother and a sister, aunts and uncles, and the usual complement of grandparents.'

'And they all live in West Virginia?'

'My father's people do. My mother's family are spread more thinly on the ground. Some of them stayed in Poland. You'll meet them all in time, I guess. There'll be a lot of talk about Casimir marrying a Britisher. They'll all come and look you over to see if you're good enough for me! Think you can stand it?'

She averted her face from the brash amusement she saw in his eyes. 'You should have taken Casimir's dreamboat home with you and given them something to talk about!'

'I don't think Amber would care for Virginia.'

'Perhaps I won't either!'

The corners of his mouth curved into a smile. 'I'm not

afraid of your being homesick—at least, not often. You'll fit in too well not to feel at home there.'

'I shall miss my parents! I've always lived with them. This is the longest I've ever been away from them!'

His glance swept over her and his smile deepened. 'Your home is in my arms,' he said quietly. 'Once I've convinced you of that, you won't be lonesome for any other. I'll see to that!'

She had no answer to that. Indeed, she could hardly breathe and her mouth was dry at the thought. How marvellous it would be when she was his wife in fact and Amber was back home in Beirut with her husband! In time Cas might even forget the Armenian beauty and she might win all his heart for herself. There could be no greater bliss in all the world than that!

They came upon the town suddenly. It lay in the fold of the mountain range, a small stream running through its centre. It consisted of a few, dark, shuttered shops, lit by circular neon strips, and a collection of dun-coloured houses that were slowly crumbling back into the dust from which they had been built. At the far end was the mosque, crowned with a tiled dome that was badly in need of repair.

'The town is far away,' Idries explained. 'Few people come this way.'

'But it looks so sad and neglected,' Stephanie murmured.

'The owner never comes here,' Idries told her. 'He lives in Tehran and cares nothing for the people here. But these things will be ended soon. The Shahanshah has brought in many reforms and there will be others to follow. One day, these people will own their own land. In my village, it is already like that.'

'They could at least repair the mosque,' Stephanie said.

'They are building a new one, near to the Rest House. That one is too close to the water. When it floods, all the walls fall down and no one can use it. The new one will be much better.'

But the old one had been a fine building in its time. It had been built on the same plan as one of the old Sassanian Fire Temples, in the form of a square cross, which had once held the sacred fire in its centre.

'Was it always so near the river?' she asked.

Idries shook his head. 'The water moved its bed in an earthquake. The earth is always moving round here. Sometimes you can feel it trembling beneath your feet, but sometimes it has bad results and people are killed and their homes fall down.'

'The people have a lot to put up with,' Stephanie sighed.

Idries smiled, his white teeth flashing in the sunlight. 'Everything is better now. We have oil now and money to do many things. Everybody can learn to do great things now!'

'Like you, Idries,' Cas put in. 'You come from a village like this yourself, don't you?'

The young Iranian nodded. 'But soon I go to university and study telecommunications. If I work hard, we will have no need to rely on foreigners any more to do everything for us. This is the Shah's wish for us.'

Stephanie wondered how it was that Cas knew so much about the young driver. Kindly though he was to those who worked for him, she couldn't imagine her father taking the trouble to find out where one of his drivers came from, or what his ambitions for the future were. Cas, she thought, was the better employer, and she felt a surge of loving loyalty towards him because she thought he was also the better man—and he was hers! She had taken on his name, casting off her father's, and she was glad she had made the change. It wasn't only because she loved him, but she was burningly proud of him as a man and a human being.

'My husband will help you all he can,' she said to Idries.

'Well, well,' said Cas, 'you said that as though you meant it!'

She felt as brave as a lion and full of conceit that she should be identified with him. 'I did,' she said.

Her courage deserted her as fast as it had come. She saw with relief that they had drawn up outside the Rest House and she leaned forward, impatient to be out of the Range Rover and able to stretch her legs. It was a two-storey building, she noticed, with the restaurant to the right of the main door.

'Yours is upstairs, honey,' Cas told her. 'If you get lost, yell for help, and I'll come and find you.'

He would too, she thought. It was reassuring to know that he wouldn't leave her to fight her own battles if she needed him. She mounted the stairs two at a time, feeling the pull of her muscles at the back of her legs and reflecting that the exercise would be good for her. She had almost reached the top when it came to her that he had gained her trust after all. Yesterday, she hadn't known what she felt about him. It had all been a glorious muddle of physical attraction and a nerve-sapping insecurity that nothing would ever change. Now, she knew it had. She knew she could trust him as much and more than she trusted herself. He might not love her with the abandon that he felt for Amber, but he cared for her, cared more perhaps than even she yet knew. It was like being hit by a thunderbolt. There was so much more to being Mrs. Casimir Ruddock than she could ever have imagined a few hours ago.

Not even the dust that had settled on her face could hide the glow that lit up her features. She was happy, she realised. Insanely, blissfully happy—and it showed! She made a face at herself in the mirror. What had she to be so happy about? And if she could see it, Cas would spot it at once. He was not a stupid man.

She put off going downstairs for as long as she felt she could and went into the dining-room, swinging her bag by its strap, and deliberately not looking anywhere in Cas's direction. She was surprised to find him alone at the table.

'Where's Idries?' she asked. That was a good, safe subject to begin with.

'He's found a friend to talk to.' He watched her through half-shut eyes as she seated herself opposite him, a small smile playing at the corners of his mouth. 'Were you hoping he was going to chaperon you?'

'Of course not,' she denied.

She could hardly contain her relief, however, when two huge plates, loaded with piles of fluffy white rice, were brought to them. Deeply buried at the bottom of the rice was a nameless piece of meat, which proved to be much more tender than she expected.

Cas was drinking beer. Her eye fixed on his glass and she felt safe enough to smile at him. 'I'll never manage to get through all this,' she said.

He grinned at her. 'You may not get much more today,' he warned her.

'We have plenty of food in the Range Rover. I'm rather looking forward to cooking under the stars. I was never a Girl Guide, or anything like that.'

'Have you ever slept out in the open before?' His tone was deliberately idle, as though her answer could only hold the barest interest for him. 'The ground can seem very hard if you're not used to it.'

She shook her head. 'I've never done anything like this before.'

There was nothing idle about the expression in his eyes. 'You're committed now, Mrs. Ruddock. You've decided to trust me after all, haven't you?'

She thought about saying that she didn't understand what he was talking about, but she couldn't do it in cold blood. Not when he was looking at her as though he were tuned in on her most intimate thoughts, and sometimes she thought that perhaps he was! 'Have I?' she compromised.

'Why now?' he persisted.

'It—it happened.' She cut off a piece of meat with hands that trembled, and transferred it to her mouth with a care that amused him. 'You wouldn't have married me unless you wanted me to be with you.'

'That was equally true yesterday,' he drawled.

'I didn't know yesterday. I thought—I knew you wanted to make love to me, and that was all I could think about. Any woman would—' She broke off, embarrassed. 'Well, a lot of them have, haven't they? I knew I wasn't the only one!'

'If you married me to cut out the competition, why did you imagine I married you?' he asked with studied interest.

This was worse than she had ever thought it could be. 'I don't know,' she admitted. 'You wouldn't have me in the office and I thought you wanted to keep an eye on me, to see that neither my father or I did any harm while you were in charge. I tried not to think about the future at all.—I didn't think there'd be any—for me!'

'I see.' He sounded unbearably sad. 'What made you change your mind?'

'You said I'd fit in with your family in West Virginia, and that my home would always be with you,' she said simply.

She couldn't interpret the strange light in his eyes and wished hopelessly that she had the same trick of reading his mind as he could hers. He reached out across the table and put his hand on hers. The feel of his skin touching hers made her heart knock painfully against her ribs.

'I'm glad you believed that at any rate,' he said. 'Though what I actually said was that your home would be in my arms—and I meant it too.' His expression softened. 'Oh, Stephanie, you little idiot! What did you suppose I was going to do with you after I'd had my way with you, and achieved your father's conviction? Put you in prison too?'

'I didn't know. Americans are always getting married and divorced for no reason at all. How should I know what you might do?'

His laughter brought her indignation to a head and she glowered at him across the table, withdrawing her hand from beneath his with an injured air.

'You've been seeing too many cheap American films, honey,' he rebuked her. 'As Amber told you, my people are good, solid Catholics, and we've never had a broken marriage in the family yet!' He put a finger under her chin, forcing her to look at him. 'Am I really such a stranger to you?'

'*Yes!*'

'And it's your nature to be careful? But now you're not afraid any more? You told Idries I'd do my best for him, so you must have come to the conclusion that I'd do the same by you, and so I will. I promise you that, Stephanie.'

'I know,' she whispered. 'Part of me always knew it, but part of me had to be convinced—'

'And now it is?'

She knew that nothing but the truth would serve her now. 'I think so. It doesn't matter any more.' She dealt

139

a final death-blow to her pride and found it much less painful than she had expected. 'I want to be your wife more than anything, you see, and I can't only be half married to you. It's all or nothing, and I want it so badly that there isn't room, for any reservations, like laying down conditions about how it has to be. I don't expect it to be perfect all the time, but I'll be with you and that's all that matters.' She met his eyes and it was as if there was nothing else in the world but the two of them. 'I'm not just in love with you,' she added. 'I love you too.'

He pushed back her fringe from her face. 'And you still think it's only a physical thing with me?'

'Isn't it?'

His smile was very gentle. 'It helps, honey. It surely helps, but it isn't the whole deal. Come on, eat up, love, and we'll be going. Are you ready?'

Stephanie slept for part of the afternoon. Cas had agreed to Idries driving for a while and had pushed her over into the window seat where she had room to curl up against him in relative comfort. He and Idries talked about the job that was in hand and for a while Stephanie tried to follow what they were saying, but the language was too technical for her to understand, and her mind soon wandered to other things, like the width of the gold band on her finger and how much its plainness pleased her eye against the smooth honey-coloured tan of her hands.

Cas's hand, shaking her awake, brought an abrupt end to her dream. In it, she had been running like a crazy thing from something that distressed her, though she couldn't for the life of her remember what it was. It could have been the hint of a woman's scent, or it could have been a chance remark that someone had made in her hearing. Whatever it had been, there was no reason that she could see for it upsetting her. But then dreams were like that. They didn't mean anything in themselves. They were no more than an outlet for the mind and didn't have to make sense.

'Where are we?' she asked.

'We're nearly there. Idries says there's an abandoned village on ahead where we can camp. One of our teams is quite close by and we can get in touch with the office over the wire.'

'Oh,' said Stephanie. She wondered why he should want to. 'I must have been asleep.' She moved into an upright position, suddenly aware that she had been making use of his arm as her pillow. 'You should have woken me before!'

He grinned. 'No need. I'd have shifted you if I'd wanted my arm back for anything.' He looked at her curiously. 'What were you dreaming about?'

'I can't remember. That was the trouble, it was something I should have remembered, but I didn't know what it was. I think it was something I smelt.'

'The usual excuse is something you ate,' he chuckled. 'What kind of thing?'

'Scent, I think. I can't remember.'

'Scent? Somebody's perfume? Like the kind Amber wears?'

She shook her head. 'Amber's is unforgettable,' she said dryly.

'Little cat,' he said without heat. 'So is Fatemeh Ma'aruf's—to me, at least! You don't wear much, do you?'

'Sometimes.' Her mouth relaxed into a smile. 'I have very expensive tastes in scent. Cheap ones can smell horrid after an hour or so—That's it! It was *cheap* scent, all cloying on the top and bitter underneath. *It was Gloria!*'

Cas didn't move a muscle. 'What was Gloria?'

'In my office. She'd been in there. It was her scent I smelt!'

'You're probably right,' Cas agreed, rather less excited than she was. 'We're going to need more evidence than that. I think we'll get it too!'

'How?'

He fondled the lobe of her ear. 'You'll find out. Good, it looks as though we're here. Do you still feel like cooking us a meal?'

She nodded. 'Something for three?'

'Something for two. Idries can sleep with the other men. I'll drive him over while you're settling in. Okay with you?'

141

She didn't say anything at all, not even when he shoved all the things she had carefully packed in the back of the Range Rover out on to the ground, heaving the camping cooker after them and opening and shutting boxes with a grand contempt for her efforts to have everything in its own place.

'There were a couple of comforters in here somewhere. Where did you put them?'

She looked completely blank, not knowing what he was talking about, and found it funny when he triumphantly pounced on a couple of quilts and dropped them on the top of the pile. She began to sort the bedding into two piles, giggling happily.

'Well?' he demanded, standing over her and looking looking at least seven feet tall.

'You'll have to teach me to speak your language—' She gasped as he lifted her bodily to her feet. 'Cas, I wasn't laughing at you!'

He touched his lips to her. 'American isn't the only language I'm going to teach you, honey. Will you be all right on your own here until I get back?'

She nodded violently. 'I want to cook something splendid and I can do that better on my own!' Her eyes misted with a new shyness. 'Will you drink beer with it?' She held her breath waiting for his answer. 'I brought some for you—'

'I'll drink wine with you.' He sighed heavily. 'I'd better get used to it! I can see I'm not going to drink much beer with you around!'

It was lonely when the Range Rover had disappeared in a cloud of dust across the plane. Stephanie spent a lot of time arranging their camp to her complete satisfaction, until everything was in apple-pie order and all she had to do was heat up the meat and vegetable stew she had ready on the gas-ring. There was nothing to do then but wait for his return. He seemed to be a long time away.

She wandered into the deserted village, crossing a rickety bridge that traversed a ravine that must have split the village into two. The spaces between the houses were only wide enough for two people to walk abreast and some of them were rutted and difficult to traverse at all. She turned to her right and came to an abrupt halt as she found herself on the very edge of a cliff which now stood bang in the middle of a row of houses. No wonder the villagers had moved out!

The back of her hands were still pricking with fright as she made her way back to the camp. She put her head down and ran the last few yards, sinking to her knees by the cooker. It was only then she realised the Range Rover was back.

'Cas, half the village has fallen over the cliff!'

'Is that all? I thought you'd met a pack of wolves at least!'

She felt better and managed a rather feeble smile. 'Two-legged ones?'

'The other kind are dangerous enough in some of these mountain passes in winter. I'll be glad if we've finished putting up all these posts by the time the winter sets in. We've had enough delays, without wolves adding to our problems.'

She blinked. 'Have you re-ordered the equipment?' she asked him.

'Not personally. I've left instructions for it to be done while we're away. I laid it on the line that this time the order had to go through without a hitch if we are to fulfil our contract. I don't intend to let our rivals in if I can help it.'

She presented him with a worried face. 'Does everyone know? If Gloria knows—Oh, Cas, supposing something goes wrong again! I couldn't bear it if anyone suspected you of anything!'

He sat back, enjoying the picture she made against the orange sky of the approaching night. 'I made a point of telling Gloria myself. As she's the only other English girl there, I didn't want her to feel that she wasn't being appreciated. Now, what's the matter?'

She pointed an accusing finger at him. 'You think she has something to do with it too!'

'I've thought so all along,' he said.

Tomorrow, he had said, was another day, but she was very much afraid it would be like the tomorrows of her youth. That was the worst part about tomorrow: tomorrow never came!

She washed the dishes and put them away and filled the kettle ready for the morning. There was nothing else she could do now, but she made a great deal of noise pretending that there were umpteen things that were claiming her attention. She felt rather than saw Cas moving behind her and turned swiftly, as nervous as a young doe.

'What do you want?' she asked him, her eyes enormous.

He reached down for her, lifting her high against his chest, and deposited her on top of the two sleeping-bags he had somehow managed to zip together. He lay down beside her and pulled one of the quilts up round her, smiling down at her.

'I want you,' he said.

CHAPTER XI

Stephanie awoke to a sense of well-being and a strong smell of coffee. She opened her eyes reluctantly and found her husband's head only a few inches from her own. His eyes were bright and full of laughter at her confusion.

'Well, my love, how did you enjoy your night in the wilderness?'

She turned over on to her back to give herself time to think up a sufficiently quelling answer. 'Very much,' she said at last. She made it sound as though politeness was everything.

Cas wasn't bluffed at all. He reached over and kissed her leisurely and very thoroughly. '*And Thou Beside me singing in the Wilderness*,' he mocked her. 'My, but what a song the girl can sing!'

Stephanie sat up and strove to restore some kind of order to the disarray around her. 'It was the wires overhead. The wind gets in them—' She found herself unable to continue. It was bad enough that he could laugh and joke about it, but she found it much more shocking to remember her own abandonment to his lovemaking. What would he think of her? Especially as she had insisted on going to sleep with her body curved intimately into his. She distinctly recalled her sleepy protest when he had turned away from her because she had wanted the warmth and comfort of the feel of him against her.

'Honey, I do know about telephone wires.'

She straightened the bedding, not daring to look at him. 'It was only because we were out in the open, and the deserted village, and the talk of wolves, and—and everything,' she tried to explain it to herself, at the same time excusing herself to him.

He hooked a lazy arm about her waist and pulled her close, ignoring her tense protest as she tried to push away from him.

'Stephanie, if you dare to belittle anything that happened last night, I'll turn you over my knee and give you a hiding you won't forget as long as you live. Now, how about kissing me good morning?'

She couldn't be sure if he meant it or not but, as her eyes met his, she thought perhaps he did.

'But—' she pulled herself together with difficulty. 'I'll I'll clear up the camp,' she volunteered.

He put a hand on her breast and smiled as he felt her thudding heart. 'Tell me first that you still love me.'

She shivered with a desire she couldn't hide from him. It was humiliating that he could arouse her so easily without once telling her that he loved her, or felt any tenderness for her. 'Sometimes I think I hate you!' she declared.

'Like last night?'

She tore herself free of him and got unsteadily to her feet. 'If you lay one finger on me, I'll—I'll sue you for assault!'

He lay back, looking up at her, his expression an enigma to her. 'Don't you mean,' he said, 'for daring to upset my wife's beloved dignity?'

'Nobody's ever—ever *smacked* me.' She looked down at him uncertainly. 'You wouldn't, would you?'

For a big man he could move very quickly. Stephanie found herself caught by the ankles and fell in a heap on top of him. His arms held her hard up against him and she had no choice but to submit.

'Shall I make love to you again now?' he asked her.

His caressing fingers on her back were very seductive. 'Somebody might come,' she havered.

He kissed her on the lips, pushing her away from him. 'You won't always have the dark to hide your real self in, Mrs. Ruddock. You're too tempting a piece for me always to wait for night to fall!' He gave her a slow, sidelong smile. 'Poor little Stephanie, you don't know if you're on your head or your heels, do you? Do you really think I'd risk bruising that luscious skin of yours? I only wanted to stop you fretting and tearing yourself to pieces because you've found out a little of what goes on inside you. Did you doubt that you were less passionate than Amber, for instance?' He spoke the name deliberately, watching her closely.

'I suppose you know all about her too?' she said,

fighting to hold back the tears. 'As if I don't know that you do!'

'Then you know more than I do! Amber has never been my mistress.'

Stephanie winced at the term. 'Why not?' she blurted out.

'For two very good reasons. One, she's very much in love with her own husband, and two, she doesn't appeal to me in that way. I like her very much, and I admire the way she's coped in the last couple of years even more. Life hasn't been kind to her, but I've never heard her complain. She's a nice person.'

Stephanie made an involuntary movement towards him. 'Fatemeh said her husband used to travel with her, but he doesn't any more. She spends a lot of time away from him.'

Cas nodded. 'They used to appear together. Then he got blown up by a bomb that went off in the street where they live and lost the use of his legs. He couldn't go on with his act, so he decided to go back to school and set up in electronic equipment instead. Amber's been supporting him until he's fully qualified. She must have told you that she's going to retire next year and go back to being a wife and, she hopes, mother. She can hardly wait to be reunited with Gregor!'

'But she's so beautiful,' Stephanie murmured. 'I don't believe she's indifferent to you. I don't see how she can be!'

Cas laughed, pulling her back into his arms. 'Idiot! Is that why you insisted on comparing yourself to Amber all the time, and always to your disadvantage? I thought you knew about her husband?'

'No, I didn't. I didn't know she was married until Fatemeh told me yesterday.' She pleated the front of his shirt beneath her fingers. 'I thought that was the reason you married me?'

'Because I couldn't have Amber?'

She veiled her eyes from him. 'Not as your wife,' she amended carefully.

He forced her head up and his blue eyes blazed into hers. 'My peculiar American morals allowing me to marry you in such circumstances, I suppose?'

'But, Cas, she's so lovely! How could I blame you for wanting her?'

'And what about yourself?' he demanded in a funny, tight voice.

'I'm your wife. It's me you're taking to America with you. I thought I could build on that. Only I was afraid too! I'm not beautiful like Amber is, and I haven't much to offer you. I've always been alone—'

'Not much to offer! Since I first saw you I haven't touched anything that hasn't been you! Even when you're out of sight and sound, you're still there inside me, driving me out of my mind because I need you so much! I had to marry you, honey, to get some peace!' He fondled her gently. 'I thought last night you knew something of what I've been feeling?'

She went as white as a sheet. 'I didn't know,' she whispered. She had only known how she felt about him. How could she have known?

'I had to keep you with me,' he went on. 'Even if I couldn't make love to you, I had to know you were there. You'll never be alone again, my diffident darling, not if I can help it! You're mine for ever!'

Stephanie flung herself closer into his arms, nuzzling her nose against his ear. 'Oh, yes please, Cas! Yes, please!'

Stephanie heard the approaching vehicles as a faint rumble in the ground beneath her. She stirred reluctantly lifting her head to see who was coming. The plume of dust in the distance told her that they were coming towards the deserted village at speed. She was immediately concerned at the state of the camp and struggled to her feet, packing things away in a sudden fever of activity.

'Cas, someone is coming! Get up! They'll think it odd to find us still sleeping at this hour!'

He chuckled. 'I don't suppose they'll find it odd at all!'

Scarlet in the face, she pulled the quilt away from him and folded it carefully, her back towards him. He shook his head at her rigid stance, smiling at the prim set to her head.

'They all knew why I wanted you to myself,' he

laughed at her. 'We could have shared their camp other-wise. *That* would have been an experience for you to remember! Have you ever slept on a *korsi*?'

'No,' she said. 'I don't know what it is.' Her prudish tones were so much at variance with the passion that still lingered in her eyes that it was impossible not to tease her further.

'It's a kind of communal bed,' he told her. 'It's made of rough boards on legs, under which is a pail of hot char-coal with a perforated lid. You sleep on it like the spokes of a wheel, with your feet towards the heat and your head looking outwards. How does that appeal?'

'Not at all,' she said primly.

'It has its points when it's cold.' He stretched himself and jumped to his feet, going over to the stove and exam-ining the coffee he had made earlier. With an expression of disgust, he poured it out on to the ground. 'Shall I make some more?' he asked her. 'What will you have with it?'

She set about folding up his bedding as fast as she possibly could. 'I like the flat bread that Idries brought yesterday, though it was better when it was crisp and hot.'

Cas grinned at her. '*A Jug of Wine, a Loaf of Bread—*' He raised his eyes to heaven. '*And Wilderness is Paradise enow!*'

It had been for her too. She stowed the bedding away in the Range Rover and came back to him. 'I'm glad we came here,' she said.

He looked up from where he was squatting in front of the stove. 'You think old Omar Khayyám knew a thing or two after all?'

She shook her head. 'He wouldn't have done for me at all. I prefer Casimir Ruddock.' She smiled shyly at him. 'It wouldn't have been paradise without him.'

What he might have said in reply was lost in the noise of the approaching vehicles. '*Aga! Khanim! Har che zudtar beya!*' The shouted words were cut off by a wave of the hand from Idries. 'Aga, Madame, we have news for you! It came over the wire for you! You must come as quickly as possible to speak to Khanim Amber! She says her husband's equipment worked very well—'

149

Cas stood up straight, shutting his eyes against the glare from the sun. 'So soon,' he said softly. 'Thank God for that!'

Stephanie jumped with sudden glee. 'Was that why she was at the office yesterday? Cas, please tell me it was!'

'She helped me set it up,' he answered. 'With any luck we'll have photos, everything, of anyone who went into your office last night. And once we know who, we'll know why!'

'Gloria!' Stephanie stated with certainty. 'But I don't see why.'

'Probably Gloria,' Cas agreed more cautiously. 'She seems the most likely candidate. Something must have brought her out here, something other than the travel which she isn't the type to enjoy. Maybe she was sent out here by someone else. Who knows?'

Stephanie was beside herself with excitement. 'A spy!' she breathed.

'More a successful nuisance,' he drawled. 'Spying is too dramatic a name for the limited amount of sabotage that's been done to us.'

'Limited? What about my father?'

'He'd lost the zest one needs to enjoy a challenge like putting this contract into effect, love, long before this happened to him. He'll be happier back in England with his wife. The company realised that some time ago. It wasn't by chance that I was available to come here in his stead. His was always meant to be a holding operation until I arrived.'

Stephanie felt more confused than indignant. 'No one told me that. Didn't they think I'd be interested?'

'I guess they left it to your father to tell you. He obviously thought you'd be better off working for someone else.' He grinned at her. 'You don't regret it, do you?'

'I don't exactly work for you any longer,' she retorted.

'Not exactly,' he agreed.

One day, she vowed, she'd have the last word between them and it would be he who retired embarrassed. That would be a day to remember! The glint in her hazel eyes told him what she was thinking and he laughed out loud, not a bit afraid. The message was clear: she could try to get the better of him any time she wanted to, he had her measure, and the seeds of her defeat lay in herself. He could overwhelm her physically any time he chose, and it was she, as much as he, who relished the fact.

Idries took a step closer to Cas. '*Aga*, you must come at once. The Khanim Amber is waiting. Do we go back to Isfahan?'

Cas nodded briefly. 'Put the rest of this stuff in the Range Rover. No, I'll drive! Hop in, Stephanie, and hold tight! Ready? Let's go!'

Stephanie giggled, thinking he sounded like the hero of an American film, but she did as he told her, bracing herself into her seat with her legs, and she was glad she had, for he took off across the rough, pitted ground with a speed she found both frightening and exhilarating. She had confidence in his ability, though, and after the first few moments she relaxed a little, more interested in what they would find when they got there than in how they got there.

'Tell me more about Amber,' she said to him. 'I wish I'd been nicer to her, but—'

Cas cast her a swift, teasing look. 'You'd better tell her. She thought you didn't like her.'

'Well,' Stephanie murmured dryly, 'I'm still not sorry she lives in Beirut. It's a long way from West Virginia.'

'Tell her that too,' he advised her. 'She'll like that almost as much as Casimir's dreamboat. She hasn't had much to make her laugh recently.'

'Where did you meet her?' Stephanie wanted to know

'Still jealous? I was at College with her husband, Gregor. He introduced me to her and he knows I've taken her out to dinner once or twice in Isfahan, in case you're wondering. Amber telephones him practically every night.'

Stephanie blinked. 'Won't he ever get better?' she asked.

'Depends what you mean by better, honey. He'll never walk again, but he manages pretty well in his chair. Amber wants him to go to England to see what can be done for him, but he wants to finish qualifying

151

first.'

'Electronics is a closed book to me,' Stephanie admitted.

'It has its uses. He sent some pretty sophisticated gadgets along to cover your office. Bugging devices, cameras that are tripped off by the heat of a body coming close to them, all sorts of things. Amber was thrilled to bits that he could fix it all up for us.'

Stephanie sat in silence for a long moment, then she said, 'Cas, it must have cost a bomb? Did the company pay?'

'My interest in clearing my wife and father-in-law is rather greater than theirs. But, if it's come off, it will have been worth it! Every last cent of it!'

'Was it very much?'

He slowed to negotiate an awkward hump in the ground. 'Don't you think you're worth it?' he teased her.

'I thought you'd made up your mind that I had to be guilty,' she confessed. 'I thought that was why you wouldn't let me go inside yesterday to see Fatemeh. Oh, Cas, I thought you didn't trust me not to do something else awful! I didn't know you'd do—*that* for me!'

'But, sweetheart, I told you—'

'I wasn't listening,' she said with regret. 'Cas, was it terribly expensive?'

'I'm not complaining—especially not if it's come off! I happen to care about my wife, little one. Too much, to have her living under a cloud of suspicion if there's anything I can do about it, no matter what the cost! Satisfied!'

'Oh, Cas!' she exclaimed. 'I wish I could do something for you too!' She put her hand on his knee. 'Thank you, darling,' she said.

He covered her hand with his own. 'My pleasure, Mrs. Ruddock.'

'Oh, *Cas*, I'll never doubt you again!' Two tears rolled down her cheeks and she brushed them impatiently away. 'I'm such a fool! I wish I'd done as you told me and trusted you to look after everything right from the start, but I'll make it up to you if I possibly can.'

He came to an abrupt halt, almost stalling the engine.

He put his arms round her and kissed her hard on the lips. 'You already have!' he told her.

Stephanie had never seen anyone make a telephone call from the middle of nowhere before. One of the men helped Cas up the nearest pole, fitting him out with a leather belt so that he could lean back and use both his hands without falling. The receiver was a more workmanlike edition of the kind that was used in telephone booths every day. Cas seemed quite at home up his pole and after a while Stephanie forgot her first anxiety about him when he had first shinned up to the top. He had obviously done this often before.

'Do we go back to Isfahan?' she asked him when he came down again.

'It would seem so.' He sounded grim and more than a little angry.

Stephanie watched him cagily, not wanting to risk turning his wrath in her direction by asking him too many questions that he didn't want to answer. 'It was Gloria Lake, wasn't it?' she hazarded.

'She was there,' he answered her. 'But she wasn't alone. There was someone else there too.'

Stephanie's eyes widened. 'Who?' she whispered.

'Ali,' he said with some bitterness. 'No wonder she found it so easy to come and go! Now the interesting thing will be to find out whom they were both working for and, after that, it will be my pleasure to sack the two of them personally.' He took a deep breath. 'Okay, Isfahan, here we come! Poor love, it isn't much of a honeymoon for you, is it?'

She looked at him with eyes that glowed with mischief. 'It'll do—for starters!' she said very much in his style. 'Is Idries coming with us?'

'I think not,' he said dryly. 'We'll have to come back again when this is all over and he may as well wait for us here.'

Stephanie found that Idries' absence had its advantages and its disadvantages. Against the incomparable advantage of having Cas all to herself, the disadvantage was that she had no excuse not to sit in the far seat from him, but perhaps that too was an advantage once the full heat of the day made itself felt in the Range Rover and any contact was almost too much to be borne.

They didn't stop for lunch on the way back. Cas bought some hot bread from a wayside baker and they nibbled it as they went along, augmenting it with the white local cheese that was obtainable everywhere.

'How about a Coke?' he asked her when she confessed that something to drink was far more important to her than something to eat.

She made a face at him. 'I have a long way to go, haven't I? Do you think they have any lemonade?'

'I'll find you something,' he promised. 'As long as you take to hamburgers, American style, you can be as English in your tastes as you like!'

He was as good as his word, bringing her back a sparkling, fizzy drink that tasted of nothing very much but which was deliciously cool against her dry throat and tongue. He opened the bottles with a flick of his wrist and then looked at her again, his blue eyes sparkling in the sun.

'Want to drive for a while?'

'If you like,' she responded. 'I don't drive as well as you do, though, so don't be too critical, will you?'

He stepped into the passenger seat, putting his feet up on to the dashboard in front of him. 'Such words are balm to my spirit! I'll take over when we get nearer to the big city. Okay?'

'Right,' she said.

It was strange to be behind the wheel of such a large vehicle, but it drove so easily that she gained confidence at every mile and she had to admit that it gave an added interest to the journey to have something to do for a while.

She stopped to exchange places with him just outside Isfahan, in sight of the bridge where he had first kissed her.

'Are you going straight to the office?' she asked. 'Will you take me with you?'

He shook his head. 'I'll take you home. This is something only I can do, honey. Do you mind?'

She tried not to let it show that she did. Women and children were always having to wait around for their menfolk, she thought bitterly. Then she thought how little cause she had to complain and managed to summon up a jaunty smile.

'I'll be waiting for you,' she said. 'I have some letters to write and I can start putting all these things away.'

The corner of his mouth twitched with amusement. 'I'll help you later on if you don't want to do them all by yourself,' he offered, knowing that she would have sorted out the muddle long before he got back to the flat.

'All right,' she said. 'I'll write to my mother first of all.'

A crack of laughter escaped his lips. 'If you do, I'll know you're in love,' he grinned at her, 'and that you can't bear to do anything without me!'

She laughed too, knowing as well as he did that she would have everything tidied away long before he would be free to help her. 'My mother wouldn't forgive me if I didn't put her first,' she insisted. 'Though heaven knows what I'm going to say to her. She'd always planned to write a special piece of music for my wedding that would naturally receive a standing ovation from all present. It would be the perfect setting for a piece of really modern church music. I should probably have hated it.'

'I can see that a certain amount of tact is called for,' he agreed, 'but I have no doubt that you'll think of something to soothe her ruffled feathers.'

She would have liked to have talked the problem over with him further, but she could see that his mind was already working on what he would find at the office when he got there. She helped him carry the extra things out of the Range Rover and into their apartment, clucking angrily when he dropped his share on the floor where he stood. It wasn't only his packing she would have to do for him, he obviously needed someone to run round after him all the time, putting his things away for him.

'Cas, must you?' she protested.

His face took on a stubborn twist to it. 'I can't stand being nagged, Stephanie. Especially not about something as trivial as the way I mess up the apartment.'

She bit her lip. It was very nearly the last straw when she wanted to go with him so badly and hated being left behind to twiddle her thumbs until he should care to come and tell her what Gloria and Ali had been up to. She turned her head away from his farewell kiss and refused to have anything to do with his departure. Why should he have all the fun, while she did all the chores?

She had only half finished putting the things away when a knock at the door interrupted her. Still feeling a little sulky, she opened the door with a frown and was astonished to see Amber on the other side—an Amber who could barely restrain herself from dancing up and down with excitement. She flung her arms round Stephanie and embraced her warmly.

'I had to come, Stephanie, to thank the two of you! Gregor has passed his exams! Better than that, the order Cas gave him has given him the confidence to start straight away in his own business! I am going home as soon as I can get a flight on an aeroplane.' She hugged Stephanie all over again. 'I'm going home and I'll never have to leave him again!'

'How marvellous!' Stephanie exclaimed, pleased for the other girl. 'Oh, Amber, I am glad! I didn't thank you either for all you did to help arrange my wedding, but—'

'But you were afraid of Casimir's dreamboat?' Amber's eyes twinkled naughtily. 'But of course you were jealous. If I had known how it was, I would not have allowed Cas to take me out to dinner that evening—'

'Nor telephoned to him on my wedding night?' Stephanie said dryly.

'Oh, that!' Amber dismissed it as being of very little consequence. 'That was for your own good! Cas told me to tell him as soon as the equipment arrived and it had to be installed at night, when there was nobody there to see us. Didn't Cas tell you?'

'No. I didn't know anything about it.'

'But, Stephanie, what did you think I wanted him for?' Amber began to laugh. 'Oh, poor Stephanie! He was so anxious that he should clear up the mystery all by himself and present you with the results as a wedding present, and then he has to hurt you like that! But then, what will you? The nicest men are frequently the most stupid! Like Cas! Like Gregor! The stories I could tell you about Gregor! But I have no time now, I must go.

When we are better arranged in Beirut you must both come and stay with us.' She smiled happily to herself, her eyes flashing with her newly restored pleasure in life: 'Our children must play together! That would be nice, yes?'

Stephanie was thoughtful after she had shut the front door behind the Armenian girl. She went into her bedroom and searched amongst her things for a writing pad and some envelopes, settling down to write the long, detailed letter she felt she owed to her mother.

She was still writing busily when Cas came in, and she looked up and smiled at him. This was his great moment and she didn't want to spoil it for him. 'How did it go?' she asked him, her voice not quite her own.

He smiled broadly. 'Industrial espionage, just like the lady said,' he told her. 'We got the contract, but they thought they'd have a second bid for the work. Both Gloria and Ali are on our rival's payroll and, from this evening, are no longer on ours. It went like a dream! I got my report off by telex tonight, and then I came straight home. Fatemeh sent you her congratulations—if such a mild word can cover her state of mind. I like your friend, little Stephanie.'

'I like yours too,' she said. 'Amber is on her way to her husband. She came to thank us, though she has nothing to thank me for. She wants us to visit them some time in Beirut.'

'And shall we?'

She stood up and nodded. 'Cas, have I told you that I love you, and how grateful I am for clearing my father—and me too? You couldn't have given me a nicer present!'

He took the writing block from her, his eyes falling to the page she had just written. His eyebrows rose. 'A motet for our first child's christening?' He gave her an amused look. 'I knew you'd think of something!' He threw the pad down on the floor and held out his hands to her. 'You're slipping, honey. Aren't you going to pick it up and tidy it away?'

She shook her head, making no effort to move at all. 'It isn't worth nagging you about. I'm sorry, Cas, that I ever thought it was.'

He pulled her closer into his arms. 'If you leave it

there, it'll still be there in the morning. Speak now, or forever hold your peace!'

She looked down at the pad and then up at him, the smile growing in her eyes. She lifted her face for his kiss and her arms crept up round his neck in total abandonment to his caress.

'Oh, phooey,' she said. 'Who cares about it anyway?'

romance is beautiful!

**and Harlequin Reader Service
is your passport to the
Heart of Harlequin**

Harlequin is the world's leading publisher of romantic
fiction novels. If you enjoy the mystery and adventure of
romance, then you will want to keep up to date on all of
our new monthly releases—eight brand new Romances
and four Harlequin Presents.

If you are interested in catching up on exciting and
valuable back issues, Harlequin Reader Service offers a
wide choice of best-selling novels reissued for your
reading enjoyment.

If you want a truly jumbo read and a money-saving value,
the Harlequin Omnibus offers three intriguing novels
under one cover by one of your favorite authors.

To find out more about Harlequin, the following
information will be your passport to the Heart of
Harlequin.

information please

All the Exciting News from Under the Harlequin Sun

It costs you nothing to receive our news bulletins and intriguing brochures. From our brand new releases to our money-saving 3-in-1 omnibus and valuable best-selling back titles, our information package is sure to be a hit. Don't miss out on any of the exciting details. Send for your Harlequin INFORMATION PLEASE package today.